WITHDRAWN
UTSA LIBRARIES

P9-ECJ-538

*The Further Adventures
of Brunhild*

The Further Adventures of Brunhild

Stories by Rebecca Kavaler

University of Missouri Press

Columbia & London, 1978

University of Missouri Press, Columbia, Missouri 65211
Library of Congress Catalog Card Number 78–50811
Printed and bound in the United States of America
All rights reserved
Copyright © 1978 by Rebecca Kavaler

Grateful acknowledgment is made to the editors of the following publications, where some of the stories originally appeared: *Perspective*, "Director's Notes"; *Yale Review*, "Further Adventures of Brunhild" and "Give Brother My Best"; *Carolina Quarterly*, "Chambered Nautilus"; *Nimrod*, "Ariadne" and "Compensation Claim"; *Phoenix*, "Stillbirth."

Library of Congress Cataloging in Publication Data

Kavaler, Rebecca, 1932–
     The further adventures of Brunhild.
     I.   Title.
PZ4.K215Fu   [PS3561.A868]   813'5'4   78–50811
ISBN 0–8262–0249–7

LIBRARY
The University of Texas
At San Antonio

The Associated Writing Programs' annual AWP Award Series in Short Fiction proudly completes its first year with the publication of Rebecca Kavaler's outstanding collection, *The Further Adventures of Brunhild*, by the University of Missouri Press.

Associated Writing Programs, an organization of over fifty colleges and universities with strong curricular commitments to the teaching of creative writing, headquartered at Old Dominion University, Norfolk, Virginia, thus adds short fiction to its already successful program bringing significant poetry to American readers via the AWP Series for Contemporary Poetry selections, published since 1974.

The Further Adventures of Brunhild was selected from among more than two hundred and fifty short fiction collection manuscripts submitted to AWP's judges. This work was chosen for publication by a distinguished group of fiction writers, including Max Apple, Jack Cady, Robert Canzoneri, Pat Carr, Raymond Carver, H. E. Francis, Paul Friedman, David Huddle, Ursule Molinaro, Speer Morgan, Guy Owen, William Peden, Natalie Petesch, Barry Targan, and Lee Zacharias. The final selection was made by Wallace Stegner, author of *The Angle of Repose, The Big Rock Candy Mountain, The Spectator Bird,* and other fine books, and winner of both a Pulitzer Prize and a National Book Award for his fiction. His foreword introduces Rebecca Kavaler's excellence to readers of this volume.

Gordon Weaver, Professor and Chairman of the English Department at Oklahoma State University, served as general editor of the first AWP Award Series in Short Fiction. In addition to two novels, he is the author of two collections of short stories, *The Entombed Man of Thule,* winner of the St. Lawrence Award for Fiction, and *Such Waltzing Was Not Easy,* and winner of the 1978 *Quarterly West* prize for short fiction.

Introduction

In Rebecca Kavaler's short stories we see, taken and vindicated, two famous pieces of literary advice. One is Henry James's counsel that a writer should try to be one of those upon whom nothing is lost. The other is Robert Frost's corollary warning that he must be able to swing what he knows—swing both in the spirit of truth and in the spirit of a game, letting the reader in but not entirely in, surprising him, delighting him, or appalling him with the unexpected which, thought over, turns out to be the inevitable.

These are stories in which obliquity is of the essence. They come on us as quietly as innocent-looking assassins in an alley, they slip into the ribs like knives while we are watching the smiler's face. For surely Rebecca Kavaler is a smiler with a knife under the cloak. Her stories are all of family relationships, the standard, everyday, tedious relationships of the blood. But in her view these relationships are always antagonistic and often savage, however they are concealed, withheld, half-admitted, or not admitted at all.

"Let's invent tortures," one of her characters says. "How about this . . . First you fill a tub with Jell-o . . ." And then, if you are Rebecca Kavaler, you sift broken glass down through the strawberry-flavored surface, dissolve strychnine into it, poise buckets of boiling water overhead, sprinkle lightly with carcinogens, and climb in cosily with mother, daughter, brother, sister, father, or son. Once in, you tie your left wrists together, and, concealing what you are doing, take knives in your right hands. And you smile, smile, look vague or amiable, as if the weapons in your hands were kitchen implements, and you had only climbed into this intimacy in order to pare carrots.

By and large, we are likely to prefer stories that are written about people whom we like and can identify with to those about people who make us uncomfortable by revealing what we do not choose to admit. Kavaler's people are not in the least admirable or lovable, and do not in the least reassure us about our own impulses. But they are devastatingly real, as carefully observed as if she had first stuck them to a cork with a pin. There they are, their legs and feelers, their multiple eyes, their curved stingers, their suggested poison glands.

It is perhaps a narrow vision—hatred concealed in banality—but how icy clear! This author can swing what she knows. Her prose is as cool as her eye, and her eye is like a surgeon's scalpel or a laser beam. With such instruments she can not only cut away gangrene, but fuse detached corneas and restore sight. Whatever we may think of the people she chooses to write about, we can have for the stories themselves nothing but admiration. The figures that spring to mind are inevitably cool and steely, but the effect is like cautery.

CONTENTS

Director's Notes for a Play
In Three Acts Tentatively Entitled
"One Man's Meat Is
Another Man's Family"

The set is the conventional dollhouse view of a two-story, six-room (not counting the halls and bathroom) interior, the front side of the house removed to give you the whole layout upstairs and down, inside and out. Stage right there is a tree, pruned away to spare the roof, which once must have tapped skittishly against the second-story windows, but branches now all to one side, atilt, like some unfortunate with a withered arm, all the way to the hedge but not beyond, not shading the neighbor's yard by a single leaf. The hedge, like the house, is cross-sectioned so you can see that the green leaves are the deceptively tender hide of a tough beast, its inner dense thicket of bare gray vines exposed like guts for anatomical study. The hedge has no virtue but vertical growth, by which time passing will be gauged. Close to the shingle sides of the house are bushes, a second line of defense. Species unknown, just bushes that never flower but put out leaves and drop them each year with no particular intent, because it is their custom. You will know that twice it is spring, once it is late fall by this habit.

Stage left is the driveway, its paving buckled and broken and showing almost as much grass as the house's narrow edging of trodden-down lawn. Poised under the kitchen window, ready for instant flight, is a light blue Chevelle, always two years old, never newer, never older, with a long deep gash the length of its right side, painted over in a blue that doesn't quite match—obviously a home job—and with signs of having been bashed at separate times front and rear.

There are references made to a garage out back, but this is out of sight. Far too short to house the stretch of a car built in the sixties, it is used solely as attics once were: to get rid of things without being guilty of throwing them away—tools, bikes, trunks, old paint cans containing the leftovers of some forgotten color, with lids so tightly glued they can never be pried off. This is the structure played up in the real estate ads Karl sporadically composes as a "roomy multipurpose garage," having in mind that it can be used for anything but housing a car. It is obvious he likes the prefix "multi"; the neighborhood, in his words, is a "fine multiracial" one, meaning, as we see, that his is the only white family left on the block, still stubbornly convinced the Expressway is coming through and it will pay better to be condemned.

Farthest left, just beyond the driveway, is another hedge, this one a traffic victim, with here and there a broken rib. Through the gaps small black, brown, and off-white children occasionally ferret their way in sneaky silence, intent upon some childish prank like placing broken glass behind the rear wheels of the Chevelle, or lighting a cherry bomb underneath the kitchen window, after which they rush down the driveway spluttering with delight. These gay feu d'artifice are apt to go off at any time, perhaps during major crises in the family life within, as when, as the end of the first act, the son, fifteen as yet and pre-Vietnam, comes home turbaned in a bloody civilian bandage, or three years later when the daughter makes her long-awaited exit from the bathroom, or even when nothing is happening at all. It is then the little pop outside detonates a major explosion within, Karl springing up from his heart-saver chair before the TV to grab his M-1 rifle from the umbrella stand by the front door, but you cannot keep a loaded gun in a house with children his wife keeps saying (the way Ellen says it makes it sound like an embroidered sampler reading Home Sweet Home) so he must direct his mad fury to the search for ammunition by pulling out all the drawers downstairs too fast too hard, spilling their contents—for the most part, used popsicle sticks which those same little children are paid to collect from the gutters and which Ellen then boils and bleaches and glues together intricately into breadbaskets—until he remembers a secret cache of bullets in his sock drawer upstairs, where the socks are neatly rolled from toe up with the tops turned over to make tidy balls, in one of which he has concealed his condoms, in the other bullets, so he pounds his way upstairs into the master bedroom, opens the door which just clears the double bed, jerks out the sock drawer and discovers the bullets are there, but the condoms are missing.

These random eruptions are for comic relief, may be inserted at the director's discretion, having no relation to the action of the play which centers inside the house. It is a one-family house, in the sense that some dogs are one-man dogs. It was bought new in the thirties, that slough of hard times between the good times of one war and the next, is now into the second generation of ownership and far too old to adapt to the strange ways of a new owner. Which means—even aside from what's happened to the neighborhood—you wouldn't get much for it if you sold it. The rooms are too small, the ceilings too low, the closets so shallow only the women's clothes can slide sideways on sagging wooden rods, the broader shoulders of the men's suits are accommodated by stacking front to back on long hooks. The walls have a rough pebble grain (the once-fashionable Kraftex) and where they have cracked with age the plaster repair has the livid slickness of a scar. Downstairs you pass from front hall to living room to dining room under squat arches, only the kitchen being granted a door, architecture reminiscent of Roman aqueducts. The stairway takes a straight narrow pedestrian route in the semi-darkness of a 30-watt bulb to the bedrooms above. One of the "many improvements" Karl notes in his ads may in fact be that bulb: in Karl's father's day—he whom the house knows now as father was then middle son of three —the wattage was fifteen. Or perhaps Karl has in mind the kitchen door. Karl's mother had known it as a heavy slab of wood that swung in and out; carrying a steaming tureen of soup she had to turn her back and push it with her behind, sometimes did not get through fast enough to miss its lethal return. The present door—a frail louvered affair that swings apart at its center and covers only the middle third of the doorway, through which you might expect to pass into either a saloon or a men's urinal—was the magazine idea of Ellen in the early days of their marriage before she was invalided, when she had many fresh magazine ideas about homemaking and cooked 101 gourmet versions of meatloaf instead of, as now, making 101 things with used popsicle sticks.

In the kitchen itself, also dating from halcyon postwar honeymoon days, when Ellen was so pretty, dark-haired and blue-eyed and plumped up with youth, Karl sinking into her at night with the drowning memory of his grandmother's feather bed, is a plastic and chrome breakfast nook, that deadly early-morning confrontation of two tall-backed benches over a formica-topped table that cries out for a push-button device for playing current recording hits.

It is here that Mrs. MacBeth is sitting when the curtain rises, writing her letter of condolence to Jackie—not that you know yet that it is Mrs. MacBeth nor even that she is a black woman, all that is visible being a pair of large feet encased in those specially molded shoes bluntly rhomboid in shape but with upper surfaces providing a detailed relief map of corns and bunions and contorted toes, shoes that cost fifty bucks a pair and shriek of the wearer's concern for saving her feet, a concern Mrs. MacBeth will voice frequently ("I can stand anything so long as my feet don't hurt," or "There's nothing worse than aching feet"), a sighing refrain that sounds like a moral maxim drummed into her at her mother's knee to which she attributes her upright way of life.

You are not surprised by her color when she comes into full view, however, since she has worked over her letter by reading portions aloud: "Us colored" she says to Jackie, a phrase that, by the third act, has darkened in her letter to Dear Ethel to "us blacks," truer to her spirit than her skin, which is pale as army khaki that has seen good service. Her hair is the color of rust and her eyes you may well suspect are light but will never know for sure because of the sunglasses. These are very dark and give her the searching blind look befitting a seer, such as she claims to be. She wears them summer and winter, indoors and out, day and night, not for effect but because, having found them in a telephone booth, she used them first for the sun and now without them—unknown to her, they are prescription lenses—she can hardly see. Not that she is unaware of their effect. She knows that when she looks at Karl and sings out in her "dreamy" voice, "Last night I had this dream . . . ," his fear is all the greater because he cannot see her eyes.

The glasses frighten Karl, but the shoes enrage him. When he walks into the kitchen he sees first those shoes. When Mrs. MacBeth enters the living room to help Ellen upstairs, his eyes follow those shoes. Rage and outrage. He knows they cost fifty bucks, and he wears the cheapest double-soled Thom McAn bluchers that Mrs. MacBeth groans under the weight of when she lifts them to clean under the bed. He confronts her directly only once: "How do you explain shoes like that to welfare?" Mrs. MacBeth makes no attempt to explain shoes like that to him. It is to Ellen she gives those long-winded, gruesome, and medically naive accounts of the vascular complications of diabetes and reports constantly on her visits to the Clinic. She wastes no breath on Karl who believes in no one's diseases (except the virus cold), to whom any disability is a hoax: the deaf mute rolling down the subway aisle with his tin can and printed plea can really hear and talk; the blind pencil seller can really see; even the amputee who paddles along the sidewalk with his torso attached to a skate-board has in some tricky fashion accordion-pleated his lower half and when he gets home can no doubt snap out his legs like Karl shoots out his cuffs. (That Ellen is crippled he believes, but then he shot her himself.)

To answer him Mrs. MacBeth relies solely on threats, in this case reminding him of his own complicity. He doesn't tell Welfare and she works for half the going rate. Should the day come when she has to keep entirely off her feet, another housekeeper will cost him a hell of a lot more. This is enough to silence him. "Her feet, my eye, it's her ass she ought to get fitted out with a special contraption, that's what she uses most around here," he says only to Ellen when Mrs. MacBeth is not in the room. Maybe Mrs. MacBeth is clairvoyant as she says she is, since upon her return she addresses her first speech to his enormous cream-colored vinyl-covered chair that can be adjusted to raise his legs to any desired height and which completely dominates the living room, making even Ellen's wheelchair seem a light frivolous period piece. "His heart, my ass, that man's got no heart," out of fair-mindedness retracting a bit, "except for that poor little thing." Meaning Ellen, soft and white as a marshmallow but weighing close to 200 pounds, and quite a job to help in and out of her chair and up and down the stairs.

The full spectrum of Mrs. MacBeth's blackmailing arts is revealed slowly as the play progresses. All we see at first is that Karl may be justified in raising hell about the telephone bill. "I have to order everything over the phone, I can't leave that poor little thing alone," is Mrs. MacBeth's excuse, but what we hear her ordering is always some way out for some niece, some nephew, in some kind of fix. Not that we sense anything ominous in those telephone calls she makes to her ex-employers; she is merely being Mrs. Fix-it, fixing law suits, compensation claims, unemployment crises, medical and dental emergencies, truancy problems, marital disagreements, housing shortages, and loan-shark entanglements. You may recognize it as just another version of the New York game of getting it at wholesale—all that has been added is soul. "There I was," we hear her, using over and over again the same telephone technique, "going out of my head, when something said your name, I heard it like I hear you now, it was the Good Lord Himself telling me to come to you." Then our ears begin to catch the cadence. "God sent me," she says, and we hear the long-ago Chicago echo of one small-time punk addressing another small-time punk: "Al Capone sent me."

But it is when she recounts a dream that it is time to pay attention. The plagues visited upon the Pharoah are as nothing compared to the misfortunes suffered by those same ex-employers "right after I had this dream," she assures Ellen, grim satisfaction in the account of fires, illnesses, divorces, heart attacks, and bankruptcies that followed immediately thereafter. At first, no one remembers for sure her dream about the President—did she really tell them the dream before he was shot as she claims: "I told you, I told you last week, there I was baby-sitting in the White House, they called me up on the telephone to come right over, it was an emergency, soon as I woke up, I knew something terrible would happen, I told you the next morning, you were just finishing up that breadbasket there, you remember I told you?" There is the breadbasket, all finished, that certainly is so, convincing enough in the end to Ellen, who convinces Karl: "She told me last week, I was finishing up that breadbasket there, she told me this dream."

No wonder Karl gives in so quickly when Mrs. MacBeth asks him to get her nephew into his union. A longshoreman's job may not be a happy one, as Karl complains, but it has its fringe benefits which have not escaped Mrs. MacBeth's darkened view. German binoculars, fifths of Scotch, French perfume litter the house—all the women stink of Chanel No. 5, even 12-year-old Julie, even Mrs. MacBeth, who gets it for Christmas. Karl's initial refusal is instinctive—he vouch for a nigger?—but when, as if changing the subject, Mrs. MacBeth turns the dark malevolence of her glasses in his direction and begins, "Funny thing, the other night, I had this dream . . . ," Karl panics. Even as he gives his promise, "I'll speak to the shop steward, first chance I get," he makes for the nearest exit, marooning himself in the November chill of the front porch, with the front door safely slammed behind him. For it is somehow part

7

of the deal, one of the fine-print terms of this kind of magic, that a dream unspoken is a dream as yet undreamed.

That porch, on the far right, marking the front entrance to the house, was screened in by Karl's father, who liked to play cards al fresco with his three sons, but Karl has never listed this as an improvement, even as a boy feeling it dangerous exposure to sit out there illuminated by electric light with his back to the night where neighbors lurked, even though then the neighbors were white and he attributed the anxious itch between his shoulder blades to insect bites. That he has forgotten this is evident when he calls up to his son (Eric is locked in his bedroom, lying on the bed, not between the sheets but with only the bedspread pulled over him and looking at the ceiling with the over-reaching lust of a fifteen-year-old).He feels in fact relief that there is no answer to his "Come down and let's play some cards," but this does not keep him from recalling with nostalgia those card games of his boyhood for the benefit of Julie, who at twelve still lies on her stomach on the floor to watch the funeral on TV, with her legs spread apart and her skirt hiked up. It must be made obvious that Karl keeps strict watch on his peregrinations as he romanticizes the past (forgetting, for example, that his father when dealing always won), pulling himself up short and reversing his march when he is only halfway down the room, in order not to find himself directly behind his daughter and looking up. Yet when she chooses the moment of his peroration, "It's taking your life in your hands to walk out on that porch now at night," to burst into tears, he is confused enough to believe that without even seeing anything he has managed somehow to violate her. This accounts for the defensive fury of his "What's the matter, what the hell's the matter?", and his blank incomprehension when she confesses it is just that the black horses are so magnificent in their trappings and Jackie so beautiful in weeds.

His warning to her, as she continues to sniffle, that she is catching a virus cold by lying on the cold floor, is the first but not the last we will hear him issue. Even when

Eric enters in the next scene with his slightly broken head and, feeling wobbly, sits down on his father's heart-saver chair and tries to explain he wasn't mixed up with any protest march of long-haired hippies—"Hell, man, I don't even know what those signs said, I just went over to speak to this chick who offered me a smoke"—and Karl yells back, "Serves you goddam right," the time having come to hand down such wisdom as can be passed from father to son, such wisdom as his father had handed down to him: "I wasn't no more than ten, eleven, just hanging around watching the firemen put out a fire, I guess some fireman stumbled over me and first thing I knew wham a billy club on my head, you know what my old man did when I got home? he took out his belt and stropped me good, teach me to be where I had no business being, he said, and goddam it he was right"—even then, spluttering, red-faced with what Eric takes as rage but is more the apoplectic intensity of a dying man in a Hitchcock thriller trying to gasp out with his last breath the great secret (the secret here being that there is no such thing as innocence), even at this poignant moment of attempted communication between the generations, Karl walks over to the window and closes it because Eric is sitting in a draft and might very well catch a virus cold.

Just as in the second act (in which Eric does not appear at all except on those thin sheets of army airmail which Ellen reads aloud), Karl chooses to worry about Julie staying locked in the bathroom so long, with the shower still running, not knowing of course that she is crouched backwards over the toilet seat, with a towel stuffed into her mouth to blot up her moans, flushing the bowl each time it fills with blood, intending to flush the fetus down too except it is much bigger than she expected and the plumbing is not too good at best (she has a vision of her father with his sleeves rolled up working away with his rubber plunger) so she wraps it up instead in the *Daily News*.

We might well at this point question both those sacred shibboleths: extrasensory perception and mother love, for neither Mrs. MacBeth nor Ellen share Karl's unrest (although Mrs. MacBeth will, when all the fuss is over and the police have left, remember a dream). At the moment, however, she is trying very hard to write a letter of condolence to Mrs. King, audible only in phrases (heavy heart . . . a father, a brother . . . all us blacks) and finding it difficult to concentrate on grief with Ellen reading to her Eric's latest letter and the baby crying in its carriage. Not that she listens to Ellen. All that is required of her is an antiphonal response when the soft thin white-woman's voice nudges: Ain't that a shame. Ain't that a fact. Ain't that the truth. Her one brief moment of attention is due to a misunderstanding. ". . . but not before he got Charlie too, right through the eyes," Ellen reads, at which Mrs. MacBeth lifts her head, incredulous: "Mr. Charlie?" But when Ellen scans the script more closely, "no-o, I guess they just call them Charlie, they call them all Charlie, I can't think why," Mrs. MacBeth loses interest. She has nephews herself in Vietnam, but they don't write letters and she doesn't know where Vietnam is. She has nieces in Washington, she knows where Washington is, it's Washington that's burning down.

And why does Ellen sniffle and shed those comfortable motherly tears over the distant death of a distant friend of her distant son in a distant war, while directly overhead her daughter tries to flush a household death down the drains? Poor Rocco, she can grieve, such a nice boy, even with that Italian name. "The only guy here who doesn't think it cornball to salute the flag," as Eric once wrote. A nice boy, who loved his country like in those wonderful Cohan and Berlin songs, and had a strong family feeling, carrying with him no *Playboy* foldouts, only a snapshot of his mom and dad and kid sister in front of some terrific Colonial suburban home, shaming even Eric into occasionally penning "What's with Julie? Say hello to Dad. All my love." Which is why she sighs, "Such a good influence on Eric," as if to say, What's a nice boy like you doing dead?

So we see it's Karl, Karl alone, who feels some indefinable oppression of the spirit, some impending sense of evil, some unaccountable malaise that makes him stalk the rooms downstairs and call up from the bottom of the staircase, "I hope you got that window closed, you stay that long in a hot shower and then you get out in the cold air, you'll catch a virus cold, Julie." For the virus is to Karl the Thing, the Blob, the science fiction fantasy of creatures from outer space that have invaded his earth, and are taking over, invisible but all-pervasive, with a malignant unquenchable yeasty growth, coming in through open windows, seeping in under the cracks in the doors, carried in with the casual caller, riding in on the kiss of a friend. Just as in the movies the puny earthlings, backs against the wall, continue hopelessly to empty their guns into the advancing evil, though the bullets plop into a bed of foam, so Karl exhorts them all, at one time or another, "Go get a shot. I'm covered by the union, go down to the clinic and get a shot."

A shot is something Karl, if not the virus, can understand. When Eric, returning whole if something less than a conquering hero, presents him with the Russian pistol taken off a dead Vietcong soldier, Karl proudly takes inventory: the M-1 in the umbrella stand, his father's old rusted shotgun last seen out in the garage, the .22 he thinks is in the glove compartment of his car but which Ellen, who likes to be taken for a Sunday afternoon airing, has removed to make room for her box of Kleenex, and now this Father's Day gift from his only son, which moves him far more deeply than he conveys with the conventional stumbling acknowledgment, "Aw, kid, you shouldn't have."

But it is important to know that in spite of his growing arsenal, only once in his life has he fired a gun (that he hit Ellen was a mistake, he was aiming at that m.f.s.o.b., that mick, that next-door neighbor when the neighbors were white who moved one door over in the afternoons). The way he tells it, even in his happy-childhood stories, he was more shot at than a shooter, having first been shot by his older brother when he was seven playing out in the garage. "He said he was aiming his air rifle at a squirrel," Karl explains, but in such a way we are left with the same doubt that may have moved him to

11

stay home when his father and the other two boys donned their gear and crept out of the house in the cold predawn mist of the hunting season. When he says the War, he means World War II, but he was no gun-toter even then, no more than a merchant seaman, at that more actively engaged—as he still bitterly, twenty years later, complains—than those hotshot brothers who worked it out in defense plants, ending up in California, leaving him—world-wide wanderer, as he thought of himself in those days—closest to the old man, to inherit his last illness and the house.

Those war stories. We get the impression his ship was torpedoed by a German U-boat on every run. But it is the time just outside Murmansk that he morbidly dwells on, admitting it's thanks to the Russians he's alive today, they fished him out just in time from the Barents Sea. So why his venomous diatribes against the Russkis and Commies, the first of which he utters even before the funeral procession has reached Arlington, before Mrs. MacBeth has written more than, "Dear Jackie, we all grieve for you in this terrible hour, it's like he was a member of the family," while Ellen is still weeping softly over John John and Caroline—"poor little fatherless children"—and Julie is admiring the widow and the horses, and Eric is blotting everything out by jerking off. "He sure goofed there with Cuba, he should have blown up the whole damn island," is not as heartless as it sounds. By his reasoning, this would have eliminated Commies like Oswald and, in some obscure way, Jews like Ruby, and Jack Kennedy would still be sitting in his rocking chair in the White House clapping his hands while his little girl danced.

But no matter how loud Karl makes his political voice, no one hears him, having heard him too often before. Ellen's glazed eyes and absent smile of consent are by now an automated response, programmed long ago, even before the children were born, when she walked through summer nights with a still new husband —it was fairly safe then, the blacks hadn't moved in, though Karl kept a wary eye out for zoot-suited types that might be wops or kikes or Puerto Ricans, who all carried knives—and she nodded agreeably and with the right timing as Karl blasted away at Truman: "Too small potato for the job, if you ask me, should have dropped the bomb on Russia back in '46, wiped the Commies out before they had a chance to make their own." It was one of the reasons Ellen had married him—she was impressed with his interest in politics and foreign affairs. Yet even in those days her mind was apt to wander, say to the question of why she was not yet pregnant—she had been brought up to believe that if you did it once you had had it and God knew they had done it more than once—and she sometimes annoyed Karl by the irrelevancy of her answers, such as "Would you rather have a boy or a girl?"

She must have first heard the story of the Great Robbery, too, on one of those walks, as we hear snatches of it whenever someone asks Karl for money—sometimes even when someone hasn't, as in the last act when Eric drives up with Rocco's sister in a black Cadillac. It's still the same story, only the amount has increased: back then, it was two grand he had wrapped up in an oilskin pouch tied around his neck—his take from being stick-man at the floating crap game that had lasted so far twenty-eight days when the U-boat struck. He had it when he fell—or was pushed?—into the lifeboat and cracked his skull. He didn't have it when he woke up in that Murmansk hospital, those goddam Commie atheistic bastards. Two grand, five, ten—he begins to sound like a Southern belle recalling lost plantation grandeurs. "If I had that dough now, if those goddam Commie atheistic bastards hadn't wiped me out, I'd have ten black Cadillacs." It should be quite clear in that final scene, when Mrs. MacBeth has settled back to write her letter of condolence: "Dear Ethel, we are all grieving in this terrible hour, it's like he was a member of the family," and Ellen is trying to remember just how many poor fatherless little children there are in this case, when Karl raises his fists and waves them in the air, calling on LBJ to put an end to this fucking war and bomb China now, he is only venting this forever unassuageable grief over his mythical loss.

No one listens to Karl, not even LBJ. Certainly not Ellen, to whom all such ranting is "man talk," time to busy herself with her popsicle sticks. (Those popsicle sticks are everywhere: in the drawers Karl searches for ammunition, in the bathroom washbasin, soaking in bleach, when Julie tries to clean off her vomit, in the fruit bowl passed as refreshment to Eric's fiancée.) Karl's complaint, "Filthy things, you don't know where they've been, I spoke to this guy who works for Good Humor, he can slip me boxes of new ones," shows that he has missed the point. This way, and only this way, she is making something out of nothing. Like babies. Something out of nothing.

Poor little thing, Mrs. MacBeth calls her, but to Ellen, Mrs. MacBeth with no babies of her own is the poor one: "Nieces and nephews are not the same thing." Note the change in her when Mrs. MacBeth wheels in the baby. She stands up to Karl, literally, her hands pressing down on the arms of the wheelchair, when he protests in his pro forma rage: "There ain't enough of those little black bastards running around outside, she's gotta bring one *in*!" There is real authority in her soft voice, even her white overfleshed arms seem firm (it may be the unaccustomed muscular effort of supporting her own weight): "*I* said she could—it's her niece's baby, she's taking care of it while the mother's at the clinic." And throughout this scene—while Julie does her business in the bathroom, and Karl, scratching himself with unease, is trying to get something else on TV besides the funeral of that nigger preacher who "asked for it, he asked for it," and Mrs. MacBeth is in the breakfast nook composing a letter of condolence to Mrs. King, Ellen keeps her wheelchair glued to the side of the hooded baby carriage so that the two vehicles look conjoined like Siamese twins and, even while reading Eric's letter, makes steady cooing noises: "Look at its little fingers, look at its little nose. They're so cute at this age. If only they could stay like this. If only they didn't have to grow up. Look at its little toes." The baby is never visible; a taped recording may be used for the infant cries that issue intermittently from the blanketed depths of the

14

carriage, for Ellen to interpret, to issue commands: "She's wet, she wants a change. She's hungry, she wants her bottle. She's tired, she wants to sleep." So long as the baby is present on the stage, Ellen sits erect in her chair; she maneuvers herself around without waiting to be pushed. Peace sits upon her brow, intelligence lights her eyes, competence moves in her hands. What the baby wants, she can give.

It is when Mrs. MacBeth wheels the baby out the back to the waiting mother that she discovers the bloody newspaper wrappings. "Every dog in the neighborhood was nosing around that garbage, so I stopped to put the cover on and this is what I found." All Ellen can say, looking at the slimy mess laid open on the kitchen table, is "See its little fingers, see its little toes, how perfectly formed, five little fingers, five little toes." It is left to Karl to discover Julie has gone, to call in the police. As Mrs. MacBeth says, she just works there, "don't ask me, I ain't a member of the family." Ellen has an overriding question of her own: "What did she *want*? What did she *want*?"

Such questions as when last seen, Karl answers, and in giving the required description, even he is vague: "She was a whore." If he means this for Ellen—he is looking at her, not the cops—he has missed his target again. She has long ago forgotten Francis Xavier O'Malley, who had begged as a little child begs. All she knows is that she was a good mother, she always kissed a child's hurt to make it well. ("Feel it," F. X. O'M. had moaned, "it's so hard, it hurts.") All she knows is that Karl is a good husband, even Mrs. MacBeth has admitted that: "One thing you have to say about him, that man's devoted to you." To which, you will remember, she agreed rather smugly: "He'd do anything for me, he would. Of course he has his little ways." All she knows is that she has always tried to accommodate herself to his little ways. F. X. O'M. had liked to see her naked, but Karl thought it shameful for her to lie in bed with no clothes on, which was why, when Karl burst in upon them, she had, out of consideration for him, reached across the bed for her robe, unfortunately at just the wrong time. "She did it to save me," F. X. O'M. had cried and Karl had wept with him, "She was all woman," and she had thought how nice, the two men holding hands. (She had remained conscious, felt no pain.)

But all she knows now is that for some reason Karl is in a rage. "If she shows her face here again, I'll kill her, I tell you, I'll kill her." (Can it be that for the rest of his life he'll have to look his whores in the face?) "That girl never could keep her mind on any one thing," is Mrs. MacBeth's summing up—as the cleaning woman, she knows this is not the first bloody mess Julie has made. "I always thought she should take up typing," is Ellen's mild judgment, but Karl's is harsher: "If I had my way, they'd all be sterilized." Offstage, Julie dies laughing: Just like the popsicle sticks. But onstage no one hears him. As Mrs. MacBeth has long ago said, "The only way to get along with that man, is to pay him no mind." Not even the cops listen.

It is possible, of course, that the children listened when they were young. A very young child might be impressed by Karl in a rage: his face turns so red, making his eyes in contrast so blue, and his coarse gray hair —blond when Julie and Eric were young—is cut short enough to stand on end like the hair on the nape of a dog ready to bite. But even small children will keep their heads under the bedcovers just so long, listening to the cold whistling keen of the bomb falling and falling but never exploding, listening to the click click click of the trigger, but never hearing a bang.

Eric, whom we leave alive and well and deep in the heart of his dead buddy Rocco's family, knows at least that when Mr. Rocco, soon to be his father-in-law, says bang you're dead, by Jesus, you're dead. That's a soldier for you, the army itself could learn. Let Karl blast the forthcoming marriage, shouting, "Hoods, gangsters, murderers," meaning "wops, dagos, spaghetti-eaters," it being not the Mafia he minds, but those brachycephalic Mediterranean types. Eric doesn't bother to answer, doesn't listen. We see him in that last act with his father's blue eyes, but colder, unlikely to fade, and blond hair just beginning to outgrow the army crop, so effulgent with the divine grace of having killed without being killed, that we can understand why Betty Rocco, down from Vassar for a weekend to hear him tell it like it was, her brother's death, never went back. Eric must have told it well: how Rocco died with his head on Eric's chest (and for all Eric knows, it might have been Rocco's head, it was hard to tell.) When Ellen gives her blessing —"from Eric's letters, I loved your brother like my own son, only a mother knows"—and presents the bride-to-be with her latest breadbasket, made long and narrow to hold Italian loaves, Eric holds Betty so that it is her head now that is spattered on his chest, he fingers her hair as a general might finger some campaign ribbon marking a great victory won over a powerful enemy with poor troops, few supplies, and in adverse weather. All he had to go on, remember, was a few brief glimpses at that family snapshot, particularly the colonial home: "That's mom, that's dad, that's the kid sister—she really looks better than that." She really didn't, must have been Eric's thought when he finally saw her, looking like the Jew-ass type he had seen in the photograph—long nose, black hair worn hippie-length, studiously dumb black eyes. Which is what Karl mumbles under his breath to Ellen when they leave: "Looks like a Jew-ass."

In answer—not that he has heard—Eric slaps contemptuously the scraped flank of the light blue Chevelle as he and his bride-to-be pick their way down the broken walk to the waiting black Cadillac. His cry of exasperation—"Look at that!" is shrill as a child's tantrum, "he's not a bad driver—never had a real accident —so why does he always get bashed in front and rear?" But there is nothing shrill in his final cry—it is the deep-throated bay of a hunter who has life treed—when he grabs Betty by the waist and lifts her high and shakes her as if he's shaking down all the golden apples of love and tells her how great he feels: "Like for the first time I got a real family."

During which exit we can still see inside the house Karl sinking back in his chair and lifting his legs at heart-saving angle, Ellen smiling up at Mrs. MacBeth, trying to draw her into a female conspiracy of delight at the prospect of little ones ("Catholics, you know, can't use anything," she smirks), but Mrs. MacBeth not having any, no thank you, her face sullen and closed. It may be pure pique—ten years she has worked in the house and Eric didn't introduce her—that causes her to say, just as she sits down at the breakfast nook and takes up her pen: "I dunno. Last night I had this dream . . ."

All this must be kept in mind as the curtain rises.

Mrs. MacBeth is seated at the breakfast nook as Karl enters the kitchen.

Mrs. MacBeth speaks:

The Further Adventures of Brunhild

Let's invent tortures, George said in bed. Exotic tortures. Margaret groaned, having found James Bond in
double-feature dose torture enough for one night. But
George went on, laying down ground rules: slow and
mind-bending, with always the promise of worse to
come. How about this, he began, first you fill a tub with
Jell-O—

But Margaret had Hilly on her mind. She said she
didn't want to play and patted his rump goodnight.
Joanna, how she would sneer at that. Margaret defended herself from that and other accusations Joanna
transmitted to her through the long-distance, short-
wave night: She had not been scared away when the
truck blew up. Three days on that kibbutz was enough.
It was the indecency of the tiny bungalow she couldn't
take, vibrating all night as if a subway ran under it.
Joanna stretching before her in the morning, her body
bragging. But after thirty years of marriage, there was
a great deal of comfort in a man's rump.

With children, you laughed or you cried. Joanna—
Margaret laughed. Conversion to Judaism, life on a kibbutz, and all. Slinging the baby on her hip and the rifle
over her shoulder. As if she were the first, as if she didn't
have great-grandparents who had done all that already
in Nebraska. Their granddaughter was a living doll,
Margaret reported back to George, blonde and blue-
eyed with a nose just like yours—George would be relieved about the nose, she knew—and Margaret had
laughed about the day-care center for the children.

Joanna explained it so patiently. The tone of voice

Margaret had once used herself, squatting on her heels in a sandpile. One doesn't throw sand at another little girl, dear. No babysitting allowed for this grandmother, George. Check her in with all the other kids, pick her up at night. Emotionally healthy environment for learning. Free of the festering sores of family life and Oedipal rivalries. Her own career fifteen years in cold storage while she stayed home with three little girls. Major in fine arts. By the time she met George she had abandoned oils, was apprentice to a sculptor. What great biceps you have, George said, like Little Red Riding Hood admiring the wolf. Into the maw of marriage and fifteen years, three daughters later, a designer of furniture. International awards. Museum exhibits. The Cannon chair now mass-produced, a household word. Not less a work of art because you can sit in it.

We're festering sores, George, Margaret reported back and laughed. Yet proudly. Proud of the rifle and the baby and the strong thighs, olive-brown, in British-style army shorts, and the joy of being up and about that made it seem always early morning of what promised to be a beautiful day. Nelson Eddy, that was Joanna. Leading a chorus of scouts through the forest, sneaking up on the Indians by blasting away with a blandly stalwart baritone. Tramp tramp tramp along the highway. That's Joanna. Now Carol was a different story.

My daughter the astronomer. Margaret said it like a Jewish mother and even George laughed. The smartest of the three—Hilly wasn't smart so much as—Now that's Hilly, all right, Margaret thought furiously, twenty-four years I've had her, my own child, and still groping for the word. And pretty. Margaret shut out the thought of Hilly, concentrated on a picture of Carol's prettiness. Tall willow of blondeness, comforting to a mother as a sniffing blanket to a child. In the small Midwestern town of Margaret's childhood, the public library had had a life-sized Grecian marble. The first piece of sculpture she had ever seen. Gleaming palely from a corner darkness in the lobby, a woman sat, long robe falling over her knees in soft intricate folds, and over her bowed head the thinnest of veils, and under that, cut in clearest perfection, the beautiful sad face. Child Margaret had stood before it and shivered with awe: a veil carved out of rock. Carol was like that. A gossamer sheer veil carved out of marble. She and her husband, astronomer too, wrote papers no one in the family could read—not even George—covered all over with the chicken tracks of mathematics. And stood in line for years awaiting their turn to peek through that big telescope in California. For Chrissake, you don't peek through a thing like that, George kept correcting her, not understanding that she used just such coy phrases to conceal the vastness of her pride.

Hilly. She was back to Hilly. And where was that? We'll see Hilly tomorrow. She must have said that aloud. She heard the firm, no-nonsense, now-go-to-sleep voice, as if she were putting the girls, not herself, to bed. But where was Hilly? Who had always known where to hide, even in a city apartment, so that no one could find her. No one. Nowhere. There were the police, searching the city streets for a five-year-old, there Margaret was, sitting by the telephone chewing the knuckles of a clenched fist, and George rushing home from the office. And there was Hilly, squatting in the laundry basket, camouflaged as dirty underwear. All those hours, motionless, not a sound. Flushed out in the end by the TV cartoons when Carol came home from school.

Margaret called out, George! Catastrophe in the middle of the night. But George only grunted in his sleep.

"I'll bet you didn't phone Hilly we were both coming down tomorrow."

She kicked him tentatively and got another grunt, which could have been yes, could have been no. When she called Hilly last week to tell her the news, she had said she would be over after the lunch at the White House. That was so Hilly could hear all about it—after all, it was not every mother who lunched with Lady Bird, along with twenty other Women in the Arts—a pride of females, George called it. Margaret had warned Hilly, "Clear everything off the floor, I'll need

21

the room to drop names." Now George had to go down too, only the day before, Thursday.

"Couldn't you see that guy in the State Department Friday, so we could fly down together?"

She should have known better. George felt it a man's role to be unaccommodating. His counterproposal was that she should drop in at the White House on Thursday. "Say you'll take pot luck." She had admitted defeat gracefully. It was worth going down a day ahead to have George with her. Things went smoother at Hilly's when they were both there. Cancel appt. with Kenneth, have hair done in Wash., she memoed herself. George, phone Hilly, she had memoed him. And he hadn't—that had been a no grunt, she was sure. She would arrive a day early, and to Hilly she would be presuming all over again to "drop in." As if she ever made the same mistake twice. With Hilly, you didn't have to. With Hilly there was an inexhaustible supply of mistakes waiting yet to be made.

Margaret could hear George in the morning: "For Chrissake, I've got to make an appointment to see my own daughter? She'll *be* there, won't she? What is there to barge in on, except the kids?" George wouldn't see it. Nor had Margaret when last year, coming back from North Carolina, she had gotten off in Washington, on sudden impulse, just because the plane made a stop there. It had seemed so simple: spend the afternoon with Hilly, see the babies, take the Pennsy up that night. Margaret felt irresponsibly gay, all spur-of-the-moment, and warmly affectionate at the thought of being a delightful surprise. Hilly's phone didn't answer, but Margaret took a cab and drove out to Bethesda anyway, figuring: she's just outdoors with the kids. And she was, in that grassy square where all the backyards of the development block were thrown together in a kitty and called the Commons.

"How did you know I was here?" Hilly gasped.

"I just took a chance, darling. Surprised?"

She was that, all right. Hilly in a rage. Like the sudden starting up of a powerful engine, a dynamo threatening to shake apart its too frail housing. Hilly with her arms crossed, containing herself, but her nails picking at the yarn of the sweater sleeves. Unraveling the sleeve of care. Joanna, Carol—that combine from the past—were hurled at her. Margaret didn't just drop in on them, Hilly bet.

"Whenever I'm flying from North Carolina to New York and the plane makes a stop in Israel or Arizona, I do just that," Margaret snapped back.

"Even if I *were* here," Hilly said—as if that were a matter yet to be settled!—"how do you know that I'm not busy, maybe Ed and I are going out tonight, and I have a thousand and one things to do, maybe I haven't got time to sit down and have one of your nice long chats." So the nice long chat turned out to be a nice long sulk, because Hilly wasn't going anywhere and couldn't, on such short notice, think of a thousand and one things to do.

I will call Hilly in the morning before we leave, Margaret decided, and pulled the covers up to her chin, as if the decision had laid her permanently to rest. Then decided again, pushing the covers off, to let George call. From him Hilly might accept it as sufficient notice. Dealing with Hilly was like being ensnarled in some terribly complicated legal document, with innumerable clauses appended in fine print.

George cried out in his sleep. Automatically, Margaret reached out and shook him down to a mumble, and the mumble subsided to a faint fluttering of his lips marking the passage of his breath. The idiot sound Hilly used to make as a child by fingering a loose lower lip. Daytime George, solid and stolid, imperturbable, let's-reason-this-thing-out George, as if life were just another hydro site, and all you had to do was locate and design the dam properly, determine the peak load, install pump reservoirs. But nighttime George, whining, whimpering, groaning. A mad laugh ha-ha-ing her awake at 3 A.M. Or a scream of pain escaping from some dungeon of torture. (Let's invent tortures. Fill a tub with Jell-O—what came next? She had never let George finish.) Hilly. Joanna and Carol had nightmares. Hilly slept like a rock. Daytime Hilly and nighttime George

—there was a pair. They would have known each other. But daytime George refused to worry.

"It's a good thing she got married when she did, and had kids one two three. She'd have been a natural for the beatnik scene—hair down to here, skirts up to there, pot, LSD, the works. All I worry about now is kid number four. Somebody in this family is bound to come up with a boy."

More of the same from Joanna and Carol. A general all-round sighing out of relief. As if a nice steady job had been found for a weak-minded member of the family they had all been afraid was unemployable.

Fiercely Margaret boxed her pillow back into shape, answering that calumny with her fists. Hilly had more in her little finger than the other two put together. True confessions at 2 A.M. More than I. Margaret had known the painful boa-constrictor squeeze of envy when she first saw Hilly's paintings. Oils. Don't touch my oils, Margaret was always saying, the girls being too young. She gave them pastels and tempera, watercolor, clay. The mess they made. So Hilly saved up from her allowance, secretly, always secretly, hiding everything but the smell of turp in her room. Margaret sniffed, but nothing ever showed. (Which showed Hilly *could* be neat, and Margaret felt resentment fresh as if just then, once again, she had picked up Hilly's litter.) The chest seemed too far away from the wall, Margaret had pushed it back a little askew, and the still wet painting behind it had slid to the floor. The dry ones were in the closet under a raincoat. Good hiding place for secrets. Half of Hilly's clothes were always on the closet floor. I will not pick up after you, Margaret kept saying. Who taught her to use oils? Secret. Who stretched the canvas for her—that she couldn't have done herself, not at that age. Secret. The wet one went back behind the chest, but Margaret stole one of the closet cache—beautiful beautiful Chagall-like thing—and submitted it for the children's show the Modern was holding that spring. Second prize, a full scholarship, and Hilly the youngest entrant. If she hadn't won, she needn't have known anything about it. None of the agony of waiting, the fear of rejection. Just the wonderful surprise of winning.

Margaret folded the pillow around her head as if she could still hear that raucous yell of rage—the heel-kicking, breath-holding kind of rage Hilly had yet to outgrow. Take them, take them all, they're yours, all of them, they're yours. Stalking out of her room into Margaret's with each one. Take that, and bam, on the floor, it's yours. And Joanna saying, but you won, Hilly, you won—Joanna who only went into rages when she lost—and Carol, whose sisterly love had jumped over Hilly—like those family traits that skip a generation—to cherish exclusively the third-born, her arm around Joanna, drawing her out of range, explaining Hilly as if she were a natural phenomenon, like lightning and thunder or falling stars: she's having a tantrum, that's all, you can't reason with Hilly in a tantrum (or lightning or thunder or falling stars).

So later all that furious secret scribbling had ended, just as suddenly, but not so loudly. Hilly was older then. Quieter. As if she had installed one of those catches on her temper, so that she might continue to slam doors with the same heavy brutal force, but they would close with just a quiet hiss. Good grades, not so startling as Carol's, but still she must have been applying herself. "She's applying herself," George said, looking pleased, his advice finally taken, "she's settling down."

"You can say that again," Margaret said, handing him the telegram. Not even to finish college, to drop out in the middle, to marry what could only be called a nice young man. Who became a lawyer, a nice young Government lawyer in Washington, D. C. A Catholic. What had happened? Was it a failure of nerve? With women it was hard to tell. They just got married.

A *practicing* Catholic, Margaret complained to George as the babies came one two three. George said she was bigoted. But she didn't mind Joanna's husband being Jewish. She could have accepted a Hindu, a Buddhist, a Muslim—anything exotic and unheard of (that is, not heard of in the Methodist-Baptist enclave of her youth). Religions of bright shimmering colors, strange off-key music, unreal as those setting-sun travelogues of

Lowell Thomas. Not connected in any way with the black bugaboo of her childhood. The old Gothic-Victorian mansion that housed some unknown order of nuns. The overlush tangled garden in front. The iron gate that so rarely creaked open and shut. The warnings whispered to little girls: don't walk past at night alone, don't ever go through that gate, no matter how sweet the blandishment, no matter how kind the face. Little girls vanished, were never seen again. Like those stories of ritual murder by Jews, George commented in disgust. No, no, Margaret corrected him, the little girls weren't eaten—although if you were little enough, there might be some confusion—they were kept prisoner, never let outdoors, underwent some strange black-magic metamorphosis to reappear, years later, as a new recruitment of black-robed nuns.

"I think she did it on purpose," Margaret told George, "married a Catholic so that she would have all those babies and not have time for anything else, not even to think."

"Forget it," George advised her, "she seems happy enough. Ed's a nice guy. He appreciates *you,* you've got to admit, so why don't you take the knife out, leave them alone."

Ed paid her compliments, if that was what George meant. Compliments never delivered direct. Via George. Or if George were not there, via Hilly, which was worse. Your wife's one dame who can wear these short skirts, George, legs like Marlene Dietrich. And, bared in a swim suit, her shoulders were pointed out to George as looking like Rosalind Russell's. Did you ever notice, he cross-examined Hilly, Margaret looks like Claudette Colbert—look at those cheekbones, that pointed chin. A collage of old releases on the Late Late Show, Margaret summed up grimly, but did not really suspect him of evil intent. He was not so subtle. The compliments were mere counterpoint to the insults he paid Hilly.

A wonderful meal, Margaret took pains to tell Hilly, the cassoulet was superb. And Ed said, "Took her two days to make, it ought to be good, she gets it out of a book, and you know Hilly, she's a slow reader." The new short haircut was even to Margaret a shock, but its severe asymmetrical lines did somehow unclutter Hilly's face, and Margaret discovered, My God, she's got a jaw of iron. But Ed said, "Reminds me of a Euclidean proof, you know the part that goes, 'which is absurd.'"

Why doesn't he ever say something nice to her? Margaret demanded of George. George said it was just Ed's way of showing affection—the way two old army buddies meet and call each other bastard. Margaret pointed out a distinction that George—and Ed—seemed to have missed. Hilly wasn't an old army buddy.

And sometimes at his most loving, he still called her Brunt. Margaret ground her teeth. Brunt. Little brown runt, Ed the new husband introduced his wife, their daughter to them. A Linnaeus, with a new system of classification, neatly fitting in a new weed. So you shouldn't have named her Brunhild, was George's defense of his son-in-law, and Hilly *is* silly. Margaret hated him for grinning, for making her grin. Carol's favorite chant—blond venomous sprite dancing around the little brown intruder, rite of exorcism, guaranteed to shrivel up a rival. Hilly is silly Hilly is silly. George had introduced the new baby to their friends with a dictum: never take a pregnant woman to the Ring Cycle. Margaret herself could not remember—even then, by the time she got home from the hospital, she could not remember—just why that name of all names had seemed the one for the new baby the moment it was delivered into her arms. Brown, not red like Carol. Not bald like Carol, but with dark long thin hair brushed by the nurse into the vanity of an old man's tonsure to hide its sparseness. One for me, now one for you, fair enough, George had said equably. Carol was him. This one was her—dark and brown-eyed, eyes truly brown, not the brown of muddy water that changes soon. And tall, too, George, Margaret had predicted, you can tell by the feet. Something had gone wrong there—just what was a mystery, with George six two and Margaret five nine and Carol and Joanna both flat-footing it to dances in fancy ballet slippers and scrunching down to fit their partners. But you couldn't call five four a runt. Not unless you lined her up with the rest of them.

I loved you best of all. More true confessions. Margaret lying flat on her back still awake at 3 A.M. It had been different with the first. No examining, no scrutiny, no questioning of love at all. The love for Carol had come in an oceanic wash, in which Margaret and Margaret's mother and now Margaret's child and her mother's mother and her child's future child all bobbed about, indistinguishable from one another, little pinpoints of life floating like plankton in a sea of love, unpent by the great breaking of waters.

(Hilly had known that with *her* first-born. Margaret and George had been ushered into the hospital room with an enormous bouquet of flowers, in the center of which George had so cleverly hidden the bottle of champagne. A Catholic hospital, of course, all alcoholic spirits forbidden, those unhygienic black robes swishing through the corridors. Hysterical laughter at George's frantic efforts to silence the popping of the cork. And trying to click together soggy paper cups. Then suddenly Hilly put her cup down and reached out her hands to Margaret. *Reached out.* Like those newspaper stories every now and then of a child run over by a car, in a coma for years, with wide-open unblinking eyes, fed intravenously, recognizing no one, then suddenly one day the eyes blink and she no longer stares at, but sees, the woman bending over her and she wets her lips and tries to speak and at last she says it. Mother. Hilly cried and Margaret cried, softly they cried together, like two women at a wedding. George said it was lousy champagne.)

That's with the first-born. But ever after, you pick and choose. Joanna, now, had left Margaret cold. Another replica of George, a little less fair, a little more weight. She sucked at the nipple stolidly, even then tramp, tramp, tramping along the highway. "You've got to be fair to Joanna," Margaret kept demanding of the two older ones. George must have noticed. He picked Joanna up more than he had the other two, played pit-a-pat with her to "Yessir, she's my baby."

But Hilly Margaret had chosen. Brunhild she had named the brown little female thing. A magnificent woman guarded by a circle of fire. And she had turned out to be Hilly. And Hilly was silly. But Margaret had consoled herself: somewhere a Siegfried awaits. The sleep is but a trance. The gods are conferring, arguing, striking their bargains. And Todd appeared. In the middle of the night, Margaret laughed.

George was right. Quite often, in the middle of the night, Margaret admitted George was right. They shouldn't have gone down to Hilly's last Christmas. It was Carol's turn to have them, and George couldn't wait to lap up that Arizona sun. Margaret had to twist his arm. "We could just stop off for the weekend, it's really on the way, and make a big do out of tree-trimming, and then I won't have to mail all these packages." So, not having wanted to be there at all, George had no right to enjoy it. "You seem to be having a good time," she said, when he came upstairs with his drink to see what was keeping her. It was an accusation. He had a glow on already and she was still unpacking, dying for a drink.

"Come on down," George said, sitting on the bed on top of the dress she had just laid out. "I want your professional opinion." Professional? Margaret hadn't noticed any new furniture. And if there were any, it would be Colonial, because that's what Ed liked, the whole damn development being Colonial by virtue of thin white matchsticks stuck in front of each pile of red brick. What they ought to do, Margaret said, is call it Williamsburg, and wear mobcaps and knee breeches and sell souvenirs. No, it was Hilly, George said. "You're the expert on Hilly, there's something different about her. Besides the hair."

"She's not pregnant at the moment, if that's what you mean."

She was thinner, George agreed, but that wasn't it. She was euphoric. Yes, that was it, euphoric. She wanted to know if there was anything special Joanna needed for her baby, she was going to send a little Care package, it looked like. And she wanted to borrow their copy of Carol's last paper, she thought she'd like to try to read it. That was hard rock going full blast downstairs, Margaret could hear it, couldn't she, and Hilly was shaking up and down and sideways and Ed was asleep again on the couch, and all Hilly did about it was sprinkle her martini over the length of him. "She said," George reported, "you have to water them occasionally or else they don't grow."

While she put on her make-up, Margaret developed a new theory. Maybe, she said, testing it on George, it's not really as boring here as Hilly makes out. Maybe she lays it all on, just for us. I can sort of see her, the minute she hears we're coming, canceling all kinds of madly gay events, warning off her real friends and rounding up those neighborhood hausfraus and Government clerks. She makes Ed swallow some beddy-bye pills, then she drags out those awful blue jeans and tee-shirt with baby-food stains, bites off her nails, rats up her hair, the doorbell rings, and there we are she's ready just in time.

George seemed to think it worthy of some consideration. "You mean," he said, after thoughtfully finishing his drink, "something like my Aunt Teresa. Whenever she heard anybody was coming over, she rolled up her oriental rugs and laid down old linoleum, because she figured they were coming to case the joint and there was nothing like old linoleum to convince them you had nothing worth stealing." He laughed, remembering Aunt Teresa. "She kept it ready, rolled up and standing on end, on the landing halfway up the stairs and God, what it took to get it to lay down again. God, it was funny. You'd let go and the whole thing would roll back up like one of those party ticklers. She had to plunk a heavy chair smack on each corner. You walked in and it looked like the furniture was arranged for some weird kind of parlor game. There we'd sit in the four corners of the room, shouting across to each other. God, it was funny."

By the time George had stopped laughing, he was asleep. Margaret corrected her theory: beddy-bye pills for any husband was gilding the lily. I'll water *you*, she

threatened, and put her dress in the bathroom to un-
wrinkle in the steam, wrapped herself in George's robe,
and headed downstairs to get the right liquid. Because
of the robe, she stopped halfway down and peered over
cautiously when she saw Hilly open the door. She
hadn't heard the doorbell ring with the music blaring
like that, how on earth could Hilly and how on earth
could those babies still sleep, or Ed for that matter—she
could see him on the couch, mouth open, shoes off.

Hilly seemed to be taken by surprise. She backed up
when he came in—a startlingly good-looking man, Margaret saw that right off, and was startled even more
when he took both of Hilly's hands in that movie lover's
gesture signifying don't struggle, you're helpless, and
leaned forward, surely to kiss her, but if so, in midair the
kiss changed direction and landed on Hilly's forehead in
a smack of Edwardian gallantry. He saw me, Margaret
thought, and continued her descent, making sure her
sash was safely knotted. She couldn't hear a word they
were saying, but they were hovering indecisively in the
doorway, and she joined them there, detouring by the
record player to turn it off.

Hilly looked flushed, but that might have been from
dancing. Margaret waited to be introduced. Hilly stam-
mered, oh Todd, this is my mother, and made it sound
as if Todd had caught her with Margaret instead of
Margaret catching her with Todd. One of those mix-
ups, Hilly explained. Todd had been going to take them
out to dinner that night, and Hilly said politely it was all
Ed's fault, she had been at—out, the night Todd called
(and Margaret remembered then she had been out several nights the past year when she had called and wondered at the stammer clipping out like a censor's scissors just where was out). Ed had forgotten to mention
the date. Just like Ed. But Margaret understood quite
clearly—from the way Hilly flicked her eyes everywhere but on Margaret's face—that the fault lay with
her: she should have been in Arizona.

Todd who? Who Todd? Hilly was treating him like
the most casual of acquaintances encountered in the
full stream of street traffic, with whose full name Marga-

ret need not be burdened. As for hers, he had to ask for it himself, which he did by advancing in so far Hilly had to shut the door, and reaching out for not one but both of Margaret's hands (so perhaps there had been nothing in that, although Hilly he had pulled forward, and her he thrust out, the better to examine at arm's length). As if the answer were Sylvia, he asked who is Hilly's mother, what is she?

"When I travel incognito, it's as Margaret Cannon," she told him, almost unwillingly, for he was stamping her with his seal of approval a little too effusively, considering that she was in George's robe. He had a penetrating eye—or was it just the anomaly of bright blue under such black hair. Nevertheless, Margaret decided, if he had looked at Hilly that way, no wonder she had cut her hair and tonight even wore a dress. A man looked at a woman that way, and up went deodorant and depilatory sales.

But he had good manners, this Todd. Refused to accept the reluctant invitation to stay for dinner. Not even for a drink. But insisted on a rain check the next night. Dinner at his place, and Mr. and Mrs. Cannon too. He looked forward to it with a pleasure that would not be denied. Margaret itched with an old impatience. Hilly was so inept at saying no. Her way was to say yes and then not show up. I'll have to check with Ed, she said, groping weakly for a way out, but Todd did not leave until she had done so, raising his black brows in heavy surprise at the revelation of Ed's presence when Hilly went over to awaken him. But Margaret wondered how long he had been aware of Ed's feet, in black hose, slim, elegant and sadly funereal, protruding from the end of the couch.

Do you really think Hilly is having an affair? Margaret asked George, but he was too grumpy about being awakened for dinner to be interested. She sent him down with instructions to pump Ed about their host for tomorrow. Hilly hadn't said a word, busying herself with setting the table. But very light on her feet now. George was right, she had lost weight. Just who is he, dear? What does he do? And where did you meet him?

Margaret had once asked questions like that, but no more. Not of a woman married five years who had three daughters of her own.

Still Margaret was glad when Hilly went upstairs early—to check the kids, she said, but she didn't come back down—and Margaret said she was pooped too and would say goodnight, making sure George was reminded by one of her "looks" that he was supposed to find out about Todd. Undressing, Margaret heard the first of several episodic bursts of typing from Hilly's room. She couldn't help wondering. Anyone would wonder. So far as Margaret knew, Hilly hadn't touched a typewriter since her seventeenth birthday. Even her letters were handwritten, a Lord Chesterfield touch in this day and age. Joanna complained: she writes me once a year and then I can't read it. Margaret waited until the typing stopped, not wishing to disturb her.

"Do you have any laundry soap in here, darling?" Margaret asked. Hilly was in the tub, the bathroom door open. Margaret heard the shower rings slide along the rod. "There's some in here, under the sink," Hilly admitted, and Margaret went in, forbearing to look, forbearing, with greater effort, even to smile at a girl hiding her private parts from her own mother. "There's a draft, dear," she said, and closed the bathroom door when she went out.

In the corner of the bedroom, the typewriter. Out of the corner of her eye, Margaret surveyed it. It was the same one, she was sure. The sleek modern portable she had given Hilly on that birthday, looking as good as new. Reams of Hilly's writing on sheets from yellow scratch pads, from loose-leaf school notebooks, on the backs of mimeographed engineering reports salvaged from George's wastebasket. Hidden in the camp footlocker Margaret had decided to give away. Margaret replaced the lid, taking nothing, saying nothing, thinking only of the perfect birthday gift, to replace the ancient L. C. Smith which had been around the house for years, whose keys must all be sticking to judge from Hilly's typing. Happy birthday, with a little card rolled into the carriage, in the format of an office memo. To: my favorite author. From: Mother.

As good as new, never having been used. Margaret detoured over the soft carpet to check the make. Straightened the pile of three-by-fives on the rickety little table. Opened the cover of a book.

When George came up to bed, Margaret gave him no chance to report. Her news came first and she bounced on the bed like a girl when she told him. Hilly's going back to school, the books were stamped Catholic U., that was Ed's doing, of course, but still back to school. She was writing a term paper, which must mean it was for credit, which meant she wasn't playing around but getting her degree at last. "She's doing it at night," Margaret told George and hugged him, as if to conduct the voltage of joy from her body to his. "If only I could help her in some way. She must be so tired, after all day with the kids and the house. This will shut Carol up, you know how she sniffs: What does Hilly *do* with herself? I tell her, wait until you have kids of your own, but she doesn't believe it, no woman without kids does." And Margaret wondered if they could give Hilly a maid. If Hilly would accept it now, a lump sum every year to pay at least a cleaning woman once or twice a week.

"Leave it alone," George said. "And don't tell Carol. Or anyone."

George was absolutely right. Not a word. And especially Hilly mustn't know they knew. You know Hilly, George, Margaret said, she'll wait until she's got the degree in her hand, and then she'll let it drop casually, or there'll be this picture of her in cap and gown—they *do* wear caps and gowns when they graduate, don't they, even though it's night school? Night school, to Margaret, would always sound like a settlement-house course for immigrant workers, but George was reassuring.

"Don't you want to know what I found out about this guy Todd?" George asked. But he hadn't found out much after all. According to Ed, a mystery guy, plenty of dough but no one knew from where or exactly what he did. CIA, Hilly liked to think, because he attended so many embassy parties and was always just back from Morocco or just off to Afghanistan. More likely a lobbyist with that kind of money, Ed thought. Kept his own horse at the riding stables Hilly used—she had gone back to riding on Saturday mornings, which was how she had met him, and the secret of her weight loss. It was no secret he had this thing going for Hilly, Ed practically bragged about it, certainly wasn't worried. It seems he makes it a threesome when he takes her out, George said, and supposed that made it all right, but he looked at Margaret with some doubt.

Where Ed was concerned, Margaret couldn't care less. Whatever was going on, it was good for Hilly. The girl was coming back to life. But Margaret did wonder which came first, the chicken or the egg. Todd or Catholic U. George couldn't care less about that, so long as Todd was chicken. Otherwise it could turn out to be a holy Catholic mess, or had Margaret thought of that? And Margaret agreed, looking very sober, the better to conceal the little licks of pleasurable excitement with which her thoughts were tasting the future. A pretty kettle of fish. Out of the frying pan into the fire. A circle of fire.

"Ed may be just a little too complacent," Margaret said with satisfaction. "If it means nothing, why does she want to keep him secret—she didn't really want us to go tomorrow night, she didn't want me to meet him in the first place. And she's kept us secret from him—it was pretty obvious she had never told him who I was."

George looked surprised. "He didn't know you were Hilly's mother?"

"You know what I mean," Margaret had begun before she saw his face. Okay, George, she said, getting into bed, that's one for you. Married thirty years, they kept score. Suddenly Margaret felt a great fatigue, sleep coming like a blacking out. Joanna, was her last thought, keeping a different kind of score.

*　　*　　*

What made you suspicious, George wanted to know, what made you open that door? No, the door was a mistake, that's all, she thought it was the bathroom.

Nonsense, said George, you were prying, Margaret. You do pry, Margaret. Carol made an observation once, which, George said, even he could follow. You are always discovering Pluto, Carol said, confirming the existence of something you have already proven in your mind.

Margaret didn't admit that. The door was a natural mistake in a strange apartment. Besides, she argued, don't they say the victim of a murder is as much to blame as the murderer, that he attracts the murderer, impels the murderer to do his deed. Come murder me, me whose life cries out? "Certainly with what you call my discoveries, George, it's the same thing. What I discover is laid out before me, calling out, discover me, discover me. Take Hilly. She could have tucked away her notes and her books and put the cover on her typewriter for the two days we are here. Instead she leaves it all lying out in the open where I'm bound to see it." (As George had left that letter from his girlfriend in his jacket pocket—but only when he was ready to break it off anyway. For two years he had been admirably discreet. Margaret never knew a thing.)

"Well, I had no idea," said George, "nor did Ed. Poor Hilly."

Not that anyone would have thought poor Hilly when they first arrived at Todd's. It was as if, her secret life fortuitously revealed, she was free to revel in it, to flaunt it, to strut about wearing Todd's gallantries like some garish feathery adornment to the simple black costume of everyday life. Todd had opened the door to them all, in equal welcome, but Hilly had advanced and taken over, him and his magnificent apartment, and the evening. It was hers. She was dressed to kill, as George put it. The short beaded dress shimmered like a sentimental recall of the twenties as she led the way to the unbroken wall of windows and flung wide her bare arms and said, look. Before looking, Margaret thought yes, she shaves now under the arms, yes for a man like that, one must shave everywhere.

But then Margaret looked, they all looked, and it was a view that stopped all thought. The apartment was cantilevered over a primordial jungle, a deep ravine of what seemed virgin American forest. Even in midwinter, without as yet snow, a thick stand of evergreens kept it fleshed out. Inside the luxury of modern furnishings, outside the luxury of life itself. "Now is that a view or is that a view?" Ed asked, in somewhat secondary proprietorship. It was a view, Margaret and George agreed.

Todd put in a modest disclaimer. "At any rate, a conversation piece," and with the accomplishment of a good host led them to sociable seating. Only Hilly hung back, still looking, and when she turned, she shuddered. "You should see it in summer. As if all this inside were a Mayan temple waiting to be overtaken and strangled and destroyed by that—that green outside."

Todd saluted her with a "darling," informed her it was only Rock Creek Park, informed husband and mother and father that he loved this girl. "The only woman I know who can find in a still life the suspense of a Pearl White serial."

No suspicion then, but yet an unease. He had an unusually good-looking face with deep clefts in cheeks and chin that made for interesting terrain. Hard to shave, though, Margaret thought, seeing already a faint dark bloom. The drinks were refilled, the conversation hummed without a jolt or a jerk or an ungainly silence. Double-entendres for Hilly; man-to-man talk with George and Ed; for her, polite attention. He was agile, Margaret granted him that. You are hopeless, all of you, she had said on the way over, I shall find out all about him. But she hadn't. How do you keep yourself busy? That was her favorite piece of Jamesian archness— What do you do? she always maintained was a brutal question. The Sunday *New York Times* occupied a large part of his week, he told her, and he always worked the Double-Crostics. It was impossible to place him. Vietnam flared up, mean and explosive, like those dirty cherry bombs the kids threw in the street, and Ed and Hilly began to shout at each other. "You mean we don't have a moral obligation to help them?" Ed threw at her, and Hilly answered him bitterly, "It's the people who want to help you have to watch out for." But even then Todd took no stand, except between the two of them, one arm around Hilly's waist, the other over Ed's shoulder, a gesture of United Nations grace.

A Negro manservant appeared in the arch of the dining area, not to announce dinner but to signal for help. From the depths of the sofa down, Ed opined, when Todd went to the rescue, "The best cooks are all men, you know that, don't you?" Margaret eyed his posture with distaste. If he slumped any more, he would be sitting on his shoulder blades. And she noticed when Todd returned how well he held himself, a man who could get away with wearing a cummerbund. He was rolling down the sleeves of his silk shirt, and his arms, strangely white under the silky coating of black hair, looked aseptic. He comes from the kitchen like a surgeon from the operating room, Margaret thought. It was straight to her he came. His next operation. "And how do *you* keep busy," he asked her, "now that your little ones have flown the nest? You must be doing something right, to keep so fit."

I have passed the physical, Margaret thought, and stretched her long legs with the confidence of middle-aged virtue free of varicose veins. I have been admiring my chair, she told him. He followed her glance to the black leather slung on stainless steel. "That's a Margo Cannon design—pure sculpture, isn't it?" he said, and it was not until then that the name struck him. "You?" He was impressed. "Hilly, you never told me," he accused her, and Hilly shrugged. "Why should I?" she said and began to eat voraciously from the platters of hors d'oeuvres.

It was then he took Margaret on the Grand Tour. They always did, Margaret was used to that. You design furniture so they show you their drapes. But it was then her unease surfaced. Lovely, delightful, very nice indeed, she said, and every room was very nice indeed, but he was anxious. Too anxious. The nervous housewife, Margaret recognized, who has done it all herself, without calling in a decorator. As if all that he was hung on whether he had good taste.

And the one room she didn't like was his bedroom. Without knowing why. Perhaps because the bed was round and she hated round beds, liking a head and a foot and a special side marked as hers. A malignant mushroom it looked, with its tufted burgundy velvet cover. Something made her look up at the ceiling, but the ceiling was white and blank and reflected nothing.

So George said that after that tour she should have known where the bathroom was. They had had dinner and she needed to go. By mistake, Margaret insisted, she had opened the linen closet door. She went back and got George on the pretext of showing *him* the place. She stationed him by the closet and flung open the door and said, "There." And when he said nothing, "Don't you see?" George said it was all very pretty, tied up in ribbons and all, but he was fumbling as for the right answer on a quiz show. "Come off it, George, if you lived alone and weren't married, would you have things like that in your linen closet, now would you?" George said he wouldn't have much of anything in his linen closet, it being all on the bed or in the laundry. Margaret lost patience. "Well, if you won't say it, I will. He's a homosexual, I don't know if he's a practicing one, but—"

And it was at that that George began to laugh. That booming big-bertha laugh of his. Because, he explained later, it reminded him of the way she spoke of Ed as a practicing Catholic. It was the laugh that brought Hilly weaving down the hall, too much to drink before dinner and then joining the men for brandy afterwards. A smile was lurching all over her face. "What's so funny?" she asked, and snuggled in between mummy and daddy.

Whenever George thought of that evening he still laughed. He had never seen Hilly really drunk before. It was disgusting, Margaret said, but George laughed. As if Hilly were still a little girl and showing a cute precociousness. To be discouraged in her presence with a disapproving frown, but alone, with Margaret, to be laughed at. "That touch football she started up, I guess we were all pretty looped, Christ, jumping all over *that* furniture—what was it that broke? A Savonarola chair, you called it?" Once started, George couldn't stop laughing.

"Those Kennedys have a lot to answer for," Margaret said grimly. "And *I* wasn't looped and *I* didn't jump over furniture."

"Okay," admitted George, "just us guys and Hilly. I could have broken my neck slipping on those damn beads from that dress of hers."

So you could, Margaret agreed with equanimity. The climax had come with Hilly's kick. Do you suppose, George asked Margaret, she meant it to land there? Never mind Margaret's answer, he winced in sympathy. Poor Todd.

Poor Todd? Poor Hilly. Ed managed to land one where it hurts too. Ed called up to give them the good news. "Guess what's with Hilly," George said when he hung up. Margaret didn't have to guess, she knew.

"What would you say the odds are, that this one's a boy?"

"You see what it means, don't you," Margaret answered him, "she'll drop out of school. She'll never finish now."

Head hanging over the bed, Margaret dosed her clogged-up sinuses. Drop, drop, drop the drops went down, tasting bitter as gall.

"And how did he sound, Ed I mean?" she asked when she was right side up again.

"Pleased," said George. "One thing you have to say about Ed, he's a good father."

"I could kill him," Margaret said. "I could kill you all."

*   *   *

And George said, "Good, dear." He hung up and told Margaret she was all wet. There had been no need to call Hilly again in the morning.

But in the cab Margaret still felt the beginning of tightness at the back of her neck. Not because she was going to Hilly's, she assured herself. The old fear of going up in a plane came back, for no reason, every now and then. George had the driver stop and picked up a *Times* before they entered the midtown tunnel.

"That's interesting," he said, neatly folding the paper into four longitudinal slices, an art she had never been able to acquire. "It says here soldiers are being returned from Vietnam at such jet speed there isn't time to diagnose their malaria, and it could become a reservoir for our native mosquitoes."

George had a knack of finding little anxiety-provoking items in the paper. She should worry now about malaria. It was not until they had buckled their seat belts in the plane that she remembered what had kept her awake all night and asked him.

"Okay, George, first you fill a tub with Jell-O. Then what?"

The Chambered Nautilus

The consciousness expands, Sidney had said when he first put his flight bag down in the Brooklyn Heights apartment. He meant the thirteen-foot ceilings. For Caro it was the wood, wood that had never been painted over. Mahogany doors. Dadoed walls. The furniture was dark grained and old without being valuable —all to the good when the apartment was borrowed and you had a kid. Where the upholstery was worn through, too soiled even for the Morrises' taste, they had tucked towels over it. Kooky couple, the Morrises, encountered casually in Greece, but all soul, off again to some place in the West Indies, address fallen behind the unmovable bulk of the nonplaying player piano, into whose guts Caro each day forwarded their mail.

Before he left for Buffalo to see his father's dying, Sidney had toured the East Village with her, reporting back to God every block how much it had changed, God it's changed, but ten years ago Caro had been a teenager from the suburbs and New York then and now was exactly the way she had pictured it. So had been Europe, India, Singapore, Greece. The map of the world was all colored in.

Sidney left, Vito called, asking for the Morrises. A new man, now there she felt a mild sense of discovery. Naked and wet from the shower, she danced to the simple rock of the early Beatles, danced under the high ceilings, up one side of the enormous room, around the embrasure of the six bay windows, down the other side, so close to the walls that her fingertips at times brushed against the waist-high paneling. Wood warm and alive to the touch, oil of wood like the sweat of a body. Tremors of pleasure moved her skin, seismographic recording of some violent inner quake.

The machine was old, a Magnavox ten, twenty, thirty years old? Old as the apartment, hundreds of years old, all old things, old people, looking alike, members of an alien race, Mycenaean artifacts. Ancient, senile, crotchety—interrupt the playing and the automatic changer hurled all its platters at you—the machine still worked, unlike the player piano and the TV console, built along jukebox lines, excavated from what era Caro didn't know. She waited for the click, the ominous rasping whirr, made a dive for the machine, and caught it just in time. But the record she wanted to put on, bought that morning, having agreed with Vito it was the greatest—the new West Coast group she had never heard of, much less heard—was where? She felt obligated to play it now, as if that would prove that his offer to take her on a trip had nothing to do with her agreeing to everything, even to getting a baby-sitter and using his pad. "He's a great kid, the greatest," so said Vito, "I really dig kids, but there's something about taking off with the little bastard looking at us—it's those bloody hornrims, why the hell don't you get him fitted with contact lenses?"

He had laughed when he said that. Vito was a loud hard laughter. Caro had lifted her behind, put the receiver down on the chair, sat on it, converting laugh to fart. His laugh was the one thing that put her off. Inside of every fat man a thin man is hiding. She had read that somewhere. Vito laughed, he had a beautiful body, but it made her wonder if inside of a thin man could a fat man be hiding.

Still looking for the record, she toweled her hair dry. She had forgotten the kid was there.

"You tell me to pull the shades down when *I* get undressed."

Propped up on the window seat, his bed by night, he hadn't looked up from his comic book. Shoes unlaced, soaked with winter slush, were firmly planted on the cushion. Along the windowsill was a meticulously aligned row of uneaten crusts from peanut butter sandwiches. Home at last in the States, the kid had discovered peanut butter.

"That's when it's dark and we have the lights on. In the daytime, nobody can see in." Defense shifted to offense. "Besides, I can't reach the damn things after you've shot them all the way up there."

A crazy sound to wake up to, Caro reminded them both. First thing in the morning, he pulled them toward his stomach and let go. Wild flailing ascent. Flapping of pull-rings against the glass. Even asleep in the bedroom, she heard it. Awoke every morning with her heart in her mouth, her body stiff as a corpse, riddled with the sound of his violence.

And besides, she remembered, better late than never, there was nothing wrong with the human body. "It's beautiful, baby, remember that. One thing I hope, you never get hung up on this nakedness bit."

Eyes were still fixed on the comic book. Ignore me like hell, Caro decided.

"Zip yourself up, I can SEE you!" she suddenly hissed.

He looked up at that. Gratified, Caro threw herself into the lampoon of offended modesty, hunching up, shrinking away, curtaining him from her sight with a pull of damp hair, lubricous as pulled taffy. Then peek-a-boo.

The kid gave his short galvanic laugh. Dead diaphragm muscle jerking to electrical stimulus in a student lab. But when she looked at him, he looked back down at the comic book. The red ball of fire had already reached the outer stratosphere, the earth was about to burn to a crisp, Gogor the robot, using his head as a drill, was boring his way up through the inside of a mountain in a last desperate effort to save mankind. He wasn't looking at her, he certainly wasn't *going* to look at her, but Caro could see what Vito meant about the glasses.

The frames were too big. Or the lens worked two ways—from the inside looking out sharpening her into focus, from the outside looking in removing his small face to a great distance. That first week at school he had brought back the form about needing glasses, right on

44

top of the form for the dentist. That was life in these United States, send your kid to school and all they can think of to do is check the plumbing and fittings. Pick them out yourself, she told the kid, you're the one who's got to wear them. So he had picked, just like daddy's. It was so touchingly square, that just-like-daddy bit. Until she remembered that Sidney hadn't worn horn-rims since before the kid was born.

Small, round metal-rimmed, that was the pair Sidney wore, picked up from a stall in the old part of New Delhi, the kind Ghandi was sometimes pictured as wearing in those sepia-tinted photos clipped from ancient Sunday supplements you saw still hanging on walls in India. Made him look as if he were just getting ready to thread a needle. She meant Sidney, but Ghandi, too. Weird, the kid choosing hornrims, out of Jungian unconscious or something. His face too seemed sometimes to be remembering his father's before all the hair. Dig Sidney, all those years he was turned on, he kept his hair short, his beard shaven. Then in India—in India of all places, when you think of why they went there to begin with—in India he decides he's graduated, he doesn't need it anymore, he's turned on permanently—it's all right for her, he says, making her feel like a suffragette who hasn't yet won the right to vote. And *then* the hair grows. Wild, man, wild, over his ears and down his cheeks, around the mouth and off the chin, no partition between beard and hair on the head, just one wild tangled wiry mess that grows as much out as down, with so much bounce it ought to be cropped regularly to stuff something. Or pack dishes in. Not until their return to New York, did she realize what he had grown to look like. Like that, she discovered in awe, seeing an old religious Jew on the subway reading a Yiddish paper.

Come to think of it, Sidney *was* Jewish, although it was something she had to come to think of. At least his parents were, though not religious, according to Sidney, nor had he ever been, but his hair sure was. Which made it all the funnier that he would be coming back shaven and shorn. On the phone last night he had prepared her for the shock. "They said it would kill Dad if he saw me like this." He sounded amused. "Since I've got their word for it he's dying anyway, I went ahead and had a haircut and a shave." Last night Caro had whooped with laughter, but now, trying to picture his return, face bare, she couldn't picture it. It was like slowly unwrapping the bandages of the Invisible Man.

Up tight, up tight, she scolded herself. She went into the bedroom to dress, grabbed a quick smoke, but what she needed was a good trip. Nothing but pot, and pretty lousy grass at that, since Sidney left, as per promise, he was so sure that without him along she would freak out for good. She wasn't sure at all that Vito wouldn't do better, the way Sidney kept putting her down, she couldn't really communicate with him any more, she couldn't get through all that hair and that put-down smile, and that noncommittal "mmmm" when she tried to tell him all she dug out of herself when she really worked with acid. Her mother used to complain that way about her shrink—all he said was either "mmm" or "mmm?" "Mmmm" was what Sidney said. She told him about the rooms, how it couldn't all be in one room, she had to go through doors, one room was filled with junk, up to the ceiling with junk, that was where she worked through her mother, sorting out the junk. There had to be another room for Daddy, empty, but the emptiness was viscous and flowing and liquid, filling up the room slowly, the flood level rising, but then she could swim, she discovered she could swim, easier than in water, in that liquid she was buoyant and nothing interfered, constricted, restrained, her limbs moved so freely. God had his room too, which she entered sometimes, but rarely. She broke into wild giggles when she tried to describe Him. Sidney said something then—he was working on a pair of sandals, trying to make them from the rubber cut from an old tire:

"Build thee more stately mansions, o my soul," he intoned, "as the swift seasons roll, leave thy low-vaulted past, let each new temple nobler than the last shut thee from heaven with a dome more vast, till thou at length art free, leaving thine outgrown shell by life's unresting sea."

It shook her, it was so much like it was. "Sidney, that's great," she said, "that's really great." He had laughed.

She sent Sidney up in a final puff, put on purple tights and a jersey shift printed in blue and red swirls like whole-body tattoo, and went into the other room, the room with the kid. She scratched his head to show that she loved him. The triumph of Gogor was veiled with the fall of her long hair, drying now to Nice 'N Easy gold.

Caro yelped, a shrill accusatory cry. "There it is, you've been sitting on it." She snatched the flat paper envelope and drew out the record, put it on to play. The rock was slower, softer, almost processional. You could hear the words. *Don't let them kid you, man, the world is really flat.* The kid laughed out loud.

"Hey, Caro," he said, "did you hear that?"

Caro didn't hear. Her face was smooth and pleasant, but deaf, dumb, and blind. She danced, she always danced when there was music, but not like before, not with naked torsion but high-stepping as in a Shriner's parade, clapping her hands together over her head in revival hallelujas. Her eyes looked closed, the slitted openings did not show through two pairs of real human lashes. When she wore those, she was dressed up. Even naked she was dressed up when she wore those.

"Hey, Caro," the kid's voice squeaked, high in sudden anxiety. "Hey, Caro." He got up and planted himself in front of her, pulling at her until she came back. "You going out?"

She looked down. Through the lashes light was fragmented. The kid was drawn in whorls. An optical illusion. "Yeah, I'm going out, is that such a big deal?"

"Where're you going, Caro? Do you have to go? I wish you wouldn't. Why do you have to go?"

He was just a kid. She had to remember that. She squatted down to be at his level.

"Look, honey, I'm just going out to play a little with Vito, not now, but later tonight, like you go out to play with *your* friends."

"I don't have any friends."

"But you will, honey, we've only been back a couple of weeks. Look at it this way, booby, how many kids have friends all over the world? That Australian boy in Singapore, Robert—"

"Robin."

"—and those English kids in India, and those Greek twins at Andros—you made friends with them when you couldn't even speak a word of Greek—and here everybody speaks English, you won't have any trouble at all."

He was a great one for correcting her, he had this thing about trivial little facts. "Not everybody," he straightened her out on that point, like this was a debate he could win on points. "Some kids speak Spanish, and the black ones I can't understand either, and they make fun of the way *I* speak."

Caro stood up. From a greater height, decisions come final.

"If you didn't hang around me so much, you'd make friends quicker."

Scream, scream, scream. Fucking old friends, fucking old place. Kids go through stages. As a baby, he was one sweet screamer. They were in Switzerland then, not for the one summer planned, but for the whole bloody year, having goofed somewhere on Lake Geneva, Evian being Sidney's guess, blaming it on the mineral water. All the time she didn't take one smoke, not even a Gauloise, or swallow one pill, not even vitamins—everyone was still scared shitless about thalidomide then —yet she felt like she was on the highs.

It was after the kid was born she hit the lows. God, how she hated Switzerland by then. She would have really blown her mind if they hadn't cleared out when they did. Twenty-four hours a day the kid cried, and all the Swiss said was, it's good for the lungs, expands the chest. They packed him like a picnic in the green canvas carry-cot. Get anything through customs tucked in his baby blanket. Shhh, the baby sleeps, and tippy-toe away the fuzz go into another compartment on the train. In Singapore he could hold his head up and bounced against her hip on a leather sling. He toddled through India, held in order by a harness, no trouble at all, except for the screaming fits when they pulled him away from the beggars or the cow shit. The stages kids go through. Like the way he had shot up in Greece, baby fat rendered off under the Mediterranean sun, running down the hill to the docks, always in shorts and cotton tee shirts that seemed to both shrink and stretch at the same time when washed. Brown thin shanks, horny knees. "Send a picture of him with those saucer eyes back to the States, we'll live off the Care packages they'll send," Sidney joked. The kid probably needed glasses even then. One nice thing, she pointed out to Sidney, he's gone off that screaming kick. Sidney had looked at him, really looked for once, made a discovery. "He's growing up!" He said it like he was amazed, the kid was Intellectually Gifted, because he no longer had to be carried or slung or harnessed or strolled, but was running about on his own two legs. But then, when Sidney really looked at anyone, anything, he was amazed by the genius of it. He walked over to her, put his hands around her neck, as if holding up a severed head, the thumbs meeting over her windpipe, fingers spreading up behind her ears, holding the hair from her face. He looked at her but the look was blind, it was his fingertips that saw, that absorbed the image of her through the whorls, the pores. Sometimes she was afraid, because of the thumbs.

Let the kid scream, Sidney said, it was a life-given right to scream. But Sidney, he turned off. You could scream and scream and Sidney didn't hear. She had screamed at the entire Swiss nation when the kid was born—six months she had done the exercises and learned how to breathe and they had said it wouldn't hurt—so when it hurt she had screamed, with Sidney right there beside her, and he had written home, first and only time, two pages of hard sell with a red ball-point pen for painless childbirth. God, how she hated the Swiss. The nurses were starched to the gills, you could see the uniforms cut out from cardboard, hung on them by folding back the tabs. But inside they were cows. Country-raw faces, and udders hanging big with milk. Clean. The Swiss are clean. But they keep dairies clean now too, hosing down the floors and using machinery of stainless steel, but the cows still stand above their shit and flick away the flies with their tails. Cows. They only let the baby try once or twice. When he gummed her, it lit a gun-powder trail of delight that crackled and sputtered all the way down her abdomen to explode in her still-bleeding womb. But then he spit her out. The nurse gripped his head and pushed it back, pushed it down, murderer smothers child in pillow, soft flaccid pillow of empty breast. Hold him so. He's a lazy one, make him work, he must work at it, hold him so. In the end they put him on a formula and bound her up, but they left the baby in her room so she could hear him cry. She was just a kid herself then. When it hurt she too could scream, but she couldn't cry. She was dry, all the way through dry.

"Oh stop that crying," she told the kid, "a big boy like you. It's not as if I'm leaving you alone. Mrs. Dana, that nice old lady in the basement, the super's wife, the one who let you in when I got back a little late the other afternoon, she'll be here. She's baby-sitting."

Couldn't get through to him while he was screaming. No use to try. Caro sat it out, sprawled in a chair, pretending to read his comic book. She used to read comic books like that when her mother brought her to the dentist, where there was always some other kid ahead, because if there was one thing her mother was, it was early, wanting always to be the first in line, even the dentist might be passing out something you had to grab up quick or there wouldn't be enough to go around.

To someone who didn't know better, downstairs, out in the hall, it must have sounded like the kid was being torn apart or eaten alive, staked out on a mound, honey poured over him and here come the army ants. She watched him—face contorted, blotched red and white, arms stiffly flailing about. It was like watching scary movies once you had learned it was all a camera trick and no one really died—fascinated horror made bearable by disbelief.

Ignored, the screams diminished to shaky indrawn breaths—it was then she felt real sympathy for him, it seemed so much like coming back from a bad trip. When there was no sound at all but the quiet juicy sucking of his thumb, she told him all over again how silly he was, Mrs. Dana was the baby-sitter, and he liked her, the nice old lady in the basement, the one who let him in.

"Hey, where're you going?" she asked, sitting up in alarm. He had zipped his jacket, was opening the door. He jumped, looked back, semiphoring her alarm back to her like a reflected signal from his glasses.

"School, it's just lunch period," he said, but after a pause, a fumble of uncertainty. Sometimes you dream you go to school when you sleep late on Saturday.

"Oh, sure," she said quickly, beamed a bright cover-girl smile at him to show she was proud he knew the time of day. It got more complicated as you got older: Greenwich, Daylight Saving, International Time Zone, Time and Life, sometimes you lost track of lunchtime.

She stood in the doorway and watched his uneven progress down the stairs, half walking, half jumping, but not until she closed the door did her heart open to him. She ran to the windows, managed to get one open, leaned out. The sun struck her hair and Danae's gold showered down. Straight below her she saw him exit, go down the stoop, foreshortened into somebody's tender drawing of somebody else's child. A garbage truck lumbered a few yards up the street, stopped in front of their building. The kid dawdled, watching the men roll the heavy cans to its rear, empty them into its grinding maw. "Hi, there," she called down, smiling, ready with a maternal incantation against evil spirits, like watch out for traffic or come straight home. He didn't hear, the iron-rattling mastication of the machine drowned her out. But the garbage man heard, looked up, whistled, laughed, waved. Heavy, middle-aged, work-grimed, his manhood called up to her and she heard him and transferred her smile. As if her body had absorbed from the wood-paneled room behind her the style of another age, she leaned further out and having kissed the fingertips of both hands, flung them out to him in the Edwardian gesture of a stage beauty acknowledging applause.

*   *   *

The doorbell rang.

It was not the first ring—she heard now the earlier rings held in some antechamber of the ear waiting this moment of attention to come through to her all at once, jostling pellmell against her eardrums, reverberating clanging hurting her head. She had not been asleep, but her legs, tucked under her, were numb from the long sitting there, leaning against the window in the classic pose of tenement dweller, arms crossed, braced against the sill, forehead pressing against the glass. The glass was in a cold sweat—she had drawn figures on it, figures that no longer held their shapes—and she felt a sudden fright, as at a missed heartbeat. It was almost dark, and she hadn't seen the dark coming. Had she missed something she would never have a chance at again, a great happening that had occurred once and for all in one late afternoon?

She opened the door on an apparition. Old woman. All old women look alike. Caro identified her with a broad smile of success: "Mrs. Dana." She almost reached out to touch the grey hair to see if it was alive. They don't make permanents like that any more, she thought. Long ago her mother's hair, when it was young and brown, had been forged by some art of metallurgy into sharp cutting waves like that. Those were the days of the neighborhood beauty parlor—before the blond frosting and the hair stylist in the City. A permanent that looked forever, renewed every six weeks. The way home from school was through the beauty shop, along an aisle of seated anonymous women, an aisle of sprung laps holding heavy purses, an aisle of mothers' hands, pinched by wedding rings, fingers dangling limp as carcasses fresh from the surgery of manicures, an aisle of slick glazed nylon legs to trip over, and fat vulgar feet or long and bony quadruple AAAA's, proud of being hard to fit, to apologize to. Somewhere in the aisle, the most anonymous of them all, she would find her mother, helmeted as if for outer space or a brain experiment by a mad scientist. The chin and mouth was all she could see. The chin would point at her in recognition, the mouth, so bitter when it wore lipstick, would smile, and the hands, caught in the act of tearing out an ad from the communal movie fan magazine—how to make your breasts grow larger, how to permanently erase twenty years from your face—would dart into the respectable housewifery of the purse and toss her the key to the front door.

Later when they had so much more money and went to Florida in the winter instead of the summer, her mother, missing afternoons, was more likely at the shrink's—father's sneer—whom Caro saw as a pink-smocked doctor, mouth pursed with hairclips, before whom her mother reclined, crying out her troubles from under the dark cavernous purring heat of a dryer turned to the temperature marked "Comfort."

"My, your hair looks nice," Caro said, childhood's good manners expressed with childhood's expletive, striking her as excruciating Gallic wit. An old woman like that, fresh from the beauty parlor, Caro would have laughed out loud except that sometimes when she was stoned, laughter rolled down her cheeks joyful as summer rain with the sun shining, but hard to explain. The old hand, nothing but bone and tendon, petted the hair —there now, see what the nice lady said about you— and Caro did laugh then. It came out of her like bubbles from an undersea diver.

"Get a paper bag," Mrs. Dana commanded, "the best way to stop hiccups, works every time."

Caro stopped laughing, moved back, not wanting a paper bag, any kind of a bag. Mrs. Dana took the move back with the door open as: welcome and come in. She shook her head. "I'd better not keep you, you're on your way out."

An order? An accusation? A prophecy? ESP? *Was* she on her way out? Caro fingered the blue serge of her cape and understood. She still had the cape on. She had used the last of the hamburger for her lunch, had gone out to buy some more for the kid's supper. "Coming in, not going out," she explained, as much to herself as to the old woman.

"Salvation Army, ain't it?" Mrs. Dana had deciphered the red initials on the cape's collar.

Caro was pleased at the recognition, pirouetted, made the blue serge swirl. She had come back without a coat warm enough for New York's winter and had suffered agony of indecision sifting through antique costumes in those new old-clothes shops: this or the Victorian English bobby's cape, or the French gendarme's or the college-boy raccoon from the twenties (the one she really wanted but Sidney didn't like the idea of wearing leather, much less fur). She had chosen the Salvation Army because of the way it swirled.

The old biddy looked shocked, a religious nut or something. "Oh come on, Mrs. Dana, it's not like they're nuns or something—is that what you're thinking?"

"No," Mrs. Dana said, "no. I don't go for that kind of salvation—tambourines in the street." But the old face stayed screwed up—even her wrinkles have wrinkles, Caro observed—not in disapproval, but the worrisome effort of putting into words what was, after all, only a vague distress. As when the doctor asked, "Now what seems to be the trouble, Mrs. Dana?" and she didn't know how to describe the intimations of mortality that goosed her on the stairs, so ended up by joking, "Old age, doctor, but they ain't found the cure for that yet, have they?"

"Maybe it's just that I'm old," Mrs. Dana said, but still she tried. "Something like that's a sign—never mind you and me we don't take to it—it meant something to them that wore it, it said something, and then you young folks come along and make the same sign say something else, and it don't seem right. What I don't understand is why you don't get some signs of your own —instead of long hair and beards like they used to wear and old clothes dug up out of other people's attics."

Mrs. Dana felt better. Always shooting off her mouth, her husband complained, but she did feel better. Not that this child—hard to believe she had a kid of her own

—had heard a word she said, standing there blinking and smiling like she didn't understand English, but speaking out always made things clearer in her own mind. In the process of saying it, she found out what she wanted to say. Magpies. They were magpies, these young ones, lining their nests with any bright-shining bauble of the past they came upon, knowing its value no more than a magpie.

"Now," she said, "what I came up for." And gave herself a shake, like a slap on her own wrist, gently reproving, and smiled. Caro watched with fascination the wrinkles fade out, fade in again in a new mix, while the old woman rattled on about knowing the old TV set up here wasn't working, and maybe he would like to come down to her place and watch for a while, she could fix him a nice TV dinner, kids seemed to go for those, no need to worry, she'd bring him up at bedtime.

She was talking about the kid. Caro felt on the back of her neck the cold breath of emptiness. The hall light was on, but behind her was darkness, the emptiness of a room left to grow dark slowly, the slow draining of its light mortal as the loss of life's blood.

"It gets dark early in winter," she said, not something said in passing on the stairs, but a cry of desperation. She fumbled, found the light switch, forced herself to turn around. The room was still empty.

"He's not back yet," she said, as if the old woman had just climbed the stairs, asked to speak to him.

Mrs. Dana kissed the air, a sound of dismay. School had been out two, three hours. One old hand clapped dryly on the other, sounding cheerfully the solution. "These kids, he's stopped off at a friend's. They never think to let you know, do they."

"He has no friends," Caro said firmly. And so she told the police, unshakable on that point. The police was Mrs. Dana's idea. Caro just stood there, stuck in the doorway, leaning against the jamb, hand on jutting hip, cape puddled at her feet, as if ready to pass an interminable time of day with a neighbor in the hall. It was Mrs. Dana who drew her back into the room and turned on the lamps and went through the motion of looking in bathroom and bedroom, all the while pressing down the front of her skirt with the palms of her hands, a habit from long years ago when she wore aprons and her hands were always busy and the first thing she did when faced with a problem was to wipe them clean of flour or water or furnace ashes or the dark loam of garden soil, a woman who did everything with her hands, even her thinking.

Back on the windowseat, Caro took up her position, but gone was the tenement watcher, arms plaited passively for chin rest. The body crouched intent, purposeful, the eyes were aimed, a sniper on the lookout for a marked victim. The street lights were on, cars passed slowly looking for a place to park. Coming home from work time. Clots of passersby appeared, ejected by the subway two blocks up. Then there was no one. She looked both ways.

"He wouldn't go that way," Mrs. Dana said, "That way's the docks." Her hands came together, squeezed hard to shut each other up.

Caro frowned over the indecipherable smudges left by her fingers on the windowpane. A Rosetta stone that would unlock the language of some long lost higher civilization.

Mrs. Dana set out on a more cheerful track. "I could swear I saw him come in—or was that yesterday. He's got such a funny way of taking those stairs, holding on to the bannister, sort of swinging from it, like he's climbing Mt. Everest and that's his lifeline. Coming down it's more like an avalanche. Better tie those shoe laces, I told him, before you break your neck. And he showed me his new schoolbag. That's a real tasshay case, I told him, looks like you work on Wall Street. But no, that was yesterday."

Caro mouthed the name of Jesus, and in the breath of his name all was lost. Like the glasses, the kid had picked out the schoolbag himself. She hadn't paid much attention, but Sidney would. That was one thing he would notice, an attaché case. He had this thing about attaché cases.

"His father had an attaché case once, a present from

his father," Caro said "but he sent it back." In the mail, registered, insured, loaded with a week's collection of Sidney's shit. The birthday present from dear old Dad, elegant bit of leather goods from Mark Cross, upon receipt of which Sidney had headed west on Route 20, two months short of a Harvard degree.

Mrs. Dana clapped her hands as if Caro had said something particularly bright. "Now why didn't I think of that? If his school bag's here, we'd know at least he did come home."

So Mrs. Dana searched the rooms again, with Caro following, aimless as a puppy, at her heels. She could have told the old woman the bag wasn't there. Because if it were, it would have been smack in the center of the dropleaf table. That's where the kid had put his things the first day he came home from the new school, and that's where he would put them as long as they stayed here. Let her move them—like last night when she had just dropped the bag on the floor to spread out her Tarot deck—and he had the screaming heebee-jeebies. She had had to put it back and clear the dishes off the dining table instead.

Follow the leader. Humped leader, old man of the sea on her back, splayed feet turned over in Red Cross shoes, clump clump clump, but busy busy clump, neither rain nor sleet nor snow having ever kept her from her appointed rounds. Caro followed, slipping along the parquet floor in little-girl slippers. It was like a treasure hunt. Caro was five and mother in the hospital and daddy who was never home was home and made a party just her and him, hid silver dollars around the house, drew her a pirate map and led her around to the hiding places, and she found them all. She held them, munificently heavy silver talismans, making all other money seem forever tiny counters in some silly game. Not clump, but clink went daddy, when she slipped along the floor in little-girl slippers behind him. Clink of ice in a glass. Even when he got up to change the TV channel, he took his glass. She woke up at night and heard the clink-clink of the sloshing drink mark his adventure down the hall and knew he was still home.

A treasure hunt. But had she hidden the kid for the old woman to find, or had the old woman hidden the kid for her to find?

"Don't go," Caro cried out.

Just down the stairs, Mrs. Dana reassured her. Knock up the neighbors, who knows, he might be right in the building, no other kids in the building but the tenants here were nice people, who knows, a door is open, the kid looks in, they say have a cookie, watch a little TV. Bony hands clasped, consulted, blue veins gorged with thought. Mrs. Dana had a better idea.

"Now why don't you do that? Knock on the doors. I'll hop down and get my coat and go up the street a piece, maybe he's in one of them stores, window-shopping for toys or something, you know how kids are, lose all track of time."

Caro protested. *"I'll* go out," but Mrs. Dana patted her hand and said, taking the precaution of laughing the kind of laugh that said don't take me seriously: "You go out, *you'll* get lost. Don't you think I can see you're knocked all of a loop, poor child."

Caro followed her to the door. Politeness. Speed the parting guest. Come again, her mother always called out, just before turning out the Colonial imitation-gas light over the carport. Do you *have* to go, the kid had asked her. She felt the old woman's skirt brush past her. Her fingers made a little snatch—what was the old woman wearing? just old-woman stuff—so slight a touch Mrs. Dana felt no more than a momentary snag, but Caro's hands hung numb from the wrist as from desperate hours of hanging from a cliff.

Old woman busily clumping down the stairs. Hop down, she said, and hop down she did. In the doorway Caro marveled, like Dr. Johnson at the woman preacher, that so old a woman could move at all. Caro blinked, feeling the stretch of her own skin, and she suddenly expanded with Olympian detachment, hangover from her last trip. Old woman, no good to eat. Caro laughed, mouth open wide, showing white strong orthodontured teeth, seemingly soundless laugh, pitched too high for human ears, but like a dog hears a dog

58

whistle, God could hear. That was how you judged people—were they good to eat? Some were fat but tasty like pork, some lean and gamey like venison, some bland but nourishing like beef or veal, some you just had to have a taste for, like mutton. But all you could do with Mrs. Dana was boil a long time for the stock.

Implosion of acid delight left her intact in the doorway. She had to knock on doors, she remembered that. What messed her mind up was not the acid, but Sidney. No meat, she couldn't even cook it for just herself and the kid. He smelled it, it made him sick. Let her gulp a White Tower hamburger on the street and when she came in he told her she had bad breath. She and the kid were on a real bat now that he was away. Hamburger or steak three times a day. He would smell it when he came back, in her sweat. The stink of meat. Let him.

There was music in descending stairs. She marveled at her own grace. Ballerina flexion of the knees. Perfect balance on her toes. It was exciting to knock on strange doors. Like taking a poll or witnessing Jehovah. Except they were to witness, not she. Have you seen my kid? Four flights, eight doors, five stayed closed. One of the fag couple was in—the one with the acne-corroded face and the forward-pursed mouth that made her hope he'd swallow it before he smiled. He hadn't seen the kid, apologized. Good news, not bad, but Caro didn't say it, she kept it friendly, smiled her thanks straight into his eyes, the color of men's oxblood shoe polish, and wondered how he kept that tanned summer-lifeguard's chest in the middle of winter, for he had come to the door topless, wearing only heavy white cotton pajama-styled pants, string-tied at the waist. He played with the string (to keep them up or to make them drop?) while worrying away at her with breathless anxious questions. She was amazed by the sudden insight: he was lonely. Lonely as those housewives whose yards she had skirted in her childhood, the ones who clung to the delivery boy, the diaper-truck man, bought Fuller brushes and the Encyclopaedia Britannica and answered with the fullness of gratitude the questions of any caller, even the female voices that came over the telephone to say,

I think you will be interested in our special hosiery sale. Caro said, at least she meant to say, that when Sidney got back from burying his father, they were going to throw one big party and he must come and bring his friend.

The nurse second floor front was in. Caro heard the hum of a machine and kept her finger on the bell, and then had to answer sign with countersign before the night latch was turned and the chain rattled free and the woman who lived alone exposed herself. Not exactly a shrinking female victim—broad shoulders, muscular calves, she blocked the doorway competently, ready with karate. Vito, passing her on the stairs, had said she was a dyke. Caro said no. Never so much as a hello, and dykes made passes at Caro, always had, which once got her square little middle-class ass all bunched up tight, but now, freed and magnified 400X, Caro found it something to brag about, the having such pandemic charm.

It wasn't exactly hello even now, just a blunt "What kid?" Readying for a date, Caro guessed, knocking her age off at something like forty, seeing her like that, deflated bag of a disconnected home dryer on her head like a revolutionary mobcap, her swarthy face washed clean, as yet unmade-up. Caro caught the sheen of a freshly depilated lip, wondered what at that age she did with a man. Sure it was man, Caro still signaled with her lashes, let her hips go limp, turned out sweet wrists with a delicate innuendo meant to stab straight through a dyke's heart. There was no response—hah! Vito. How beautiful people were once you got them to open the door and show themselves. It had gotten through to this one about the kid, and she stepped out into the hall, answering a professional call, squaring off against disaster with the practical presence of someone manually skilled (someone warned when young to learn a good trade and who had done so). Willing to take over the search herself, but brought up short, tied umbilically to her previous plans by the dangling plastic hose of the dryer. Anything she could do, let her know, and Caro nodded, meek as a patient, and asked her to come too.

The mod pair—we've got another young marrieds on the second floor, Mrs. Dana had told her, grimacing cutely when she first moved in—were already out in the hall, having heard something was going on. They made quite a chorus of their concern, but Caro kept biting back ff—ff—ff— sounds of contempt, seeing through their open door into the elegance of a marble-paved foyer decorated with psychedelic art in which she saw them posing for the *Sunday Times* magazine all dressed up in their Lord and Taylor version of hippie high fashion, His and Hers. Can't you get any signs of your own? she all but asked. Once, *once,* at some New Year's Eve ball, they had no doubt smoked one joint between them —look Ma, we're really grooving—puffing at it with the giggling expectancy due a Broadway novelty item, a practical joke cigar reputed to explode harmlessly but with a big bang. And living off it ever since: oh, we've been through that, Caro could hear them saying, dismissing pot, implying they were now on to something better, like making TV commercials or computer programming or free-lancing to order for *McCalls* and *Redbook.* But they too were part of this commune of love, through which the stairs descended like a small-town Main Street, onto which doors opened and faces smiled and people said, come in and can we help you?, the odor of goodness wafting down the halls and staircase sweeter, more pungent than any dinner cooking, making her eyes water. Goodness made her cry. Not pain. Not hurt. She had never cried at the sight of her father, puking into the toilet bowl—when he could make it that far—Noah exposing himself naked before his child. No Ham this child, but a good little girl who approached walking backwards and covered him up. She had never cried when her mother left and came back and left and came back, each time swearing she had had it up to here, this was it, packing as thoroughly as if she were vacating a hotel room, checking the emptiness of drawers, stripping the closet bare so that the metal hangers swayed like a forest chemically defoliated that would never bloom with clothes again.

But old movies could make her cry. The ones made

a long time ago, in the long-skirted thirties, that you caught on TV: the old corny Charlie-Chaplin-plotted but without the funny stuff movies, scored for strings, where somebody was always giving up something for somebody else—mother for child, man for woman, woman for man, soldier for buddy—oh the goodness of them all. Or strangers on a street, just being kind to one another. Like the first night they were back in New York, she and Sidney and the kid had walked about making like Brooklyn was just another foreign country —funny to think to the kid it was, and in some ways even to them. "Hey, dig that, Sidney, they got a state lottery now," she had just finished saying, but without any particular delight because the staid geometric de-emotionalized sign made you feel it was more like making a bank deposit than taking a fling on a fortune— when they saw the cop bending over the alky, the genuine Bowery-bum article, sprawled in a doorway between the two stores. On your feet, Mac, I gotta take you in, the cop said, and Sidney stopped. "Why don't you leave him alone, he's not hurting anyone." The cop straightened up and stuck his Irish-pig face into Sidney's—the kind of meaty cut of a face that made Sidney want to vomit—and roared like a bull, really like a bull, bull jabbed by picador, pierced by banderillos: "You want the poor bastard to freeze to death?" At the end of the block, Caro had started to cry: love was so beautiful and brief and unexpected, a falling star, someone said look and it was already gone. Like now, she went down the stairs and met it at every landing, everyone worried about the kid—

On ground level, where the stairs ended, leaning cheek to cheek against the newel, she pensively wept, delighted with the rainbow refraction of light through those lashes, until Mrs. Dana came in, hunched against the cold, and took her arm and led her back upstairs, gasping out phrases turned for comfort, her breathing sounding like a high-altitude effort. "Supper time, you'll see. They all turn up around supper time. Can't hear you or me, but stomach tells them it's time to go home. They hear that all right."

"Oh, I know that," Caro said, and stopped crying out of annoyance. She shook herself free and ran lightly to her landing, waiting there for the old woman to hike herself up along the bannister. "Oh, did I tell you?" she asked downward, the question promising a message, some bit of news, delivered during Mrs. Dana's absence. Her hair, having found its middle part, swung forward, leaving visible only a thin slice of her face, the triumphant tip of her nose, the complacent roundness of chin. "He can swim like a fish."

Not in that water, not this time of the year. But Mrs. Dana spoke low, not to be heard. "Don't it bother you, all that hair?" she asked, reaching at last the same level. "Ain't it hot in summer on the back of your neck? Funny thing, when I was a girl, we couldn't wait to be old enough to put it up. But then, come to think of it, first thing you know we were saying to each other, come on, let your hair down: Boy, we'd say, I had a coupla drinks and really let my hair down. Boy, we said. Man, you say." Caro had left her door open and Mrs. Dana went in, sat down, finished her thought while unbuttoning her coat, the words measured like some tinker tailor soldier sailor button-counting rhyme: Top button, "Tell it like it is, you say—read that in the papers all the time now." Middle button, "Guess you gotta say something different." Bottom and last, "You already got your hair down."

Soundless rictus of a laugh. She looks like a monkey, Caro thought. A chimp, the kid would have corrected her, being particular about species. And the way her ears stick out. Now she's meditating, she's going to scratch for fleas.

"Call the police," Mrs. Dana said.

Caro laughed, loose free trilling laughter, tossing her hair back. You didn't *call* the police. Don't call us, we'll call you. Mrs. Dana's hand readied itself to slap, but Caro picked up the phone, holding a strange black instrument of unknown purpose. Which end to put to the mouth, which to the ear?

It was Mrs. Dana who made the call. At the approaching thud of official feet, Caro panicked, went into the bedroom and lit a stick of incense. Takes me back, Mrs. Dana said, sniffing as she answered the door: joss sticks, mahjong, beaded curtains.

There were two of them. Caro felt free to stare, there was a one-way mirror, she could see them, they couldn't see her. "You the mama?" the fat one asked, doubting it. Don't they have to pass a physical, it occurred to Caro. The other one was younger, thinner, bony ridges of cheek and nose still red from the cold. The way he stared at her, the mirror was one way his way. Carelessly she folded up her legs, sat on them.

"She's all shook up," Mrs. Dana said and answered for her. She knew all the answers, even where Sidney was, Caro wondered how. Friends? Caro spoke up at that: the kid had no friends. And she shook her head no when they asked if he hung out around the docks, smiling at the secret she shared with the kid: he could swim like a fish. She saw him for a flash, in the Mediterranean sun, skinny legs jogging like pistons, running down the hill to the blue water, the belly-whopper of his dive.

Don't you worry, the fat one said. He closed his black book, a clerk finished taking an order. "Hundred to one he's right in the neighborhood. Just moved in, a kid that age turns the wrong way at a corner, right away he's lost. We'll find him. It's these older ones that run away, these hippie types, they give us trouble."

Until then, the young one said nothing, leaned backwards against the table where the kid's schoolbag should have been. Old dropleaf, weak in the legs. It creaked as he kept easing up, shifting his weight, leaning back. Without looking, Caro felt the slow rocking rhythm of his alternating pressure, the bearing down, the easing up. Ready to go, he brought his visored hat down, and slapped it against the table, before adjusting it carefully on his head.

"Who'd run away from a mama like that, eh Joe?"

What buddy Joe said back, Caro couldn't hear but they both laughed, moving to the door. Fat-assed clumsy walk viewed from the rear, both of them, even the thin one. Maybe that was the hobble of a gunbelt and a holster slapping always against the thigh. They ought to be mounted, Caro decided, on bikes, on horses. On foot they were a species out of its natural element, ludicrous like seals flopping on shore.

The bell rang before they had the door opened. "There he is, like I said," Mrs. Dana said, half-shrugging off her coat as if relief had come in a sudden hot flush. The two cops nodded, grinned at each other, made their faces official and serious before turning the knob. But it wasn't the kid, it was the fag from down below, and it wasn't pajamas he had been wearing, Caro saw now, but the bottom half of a Judo outfit, seeing the heavy white cotton jacket tied at his waist with a belt dyed a not-to-be-believed purple-black. At the onslaught of police, he shrank back, clutching a silver pitcher steaming aromatically.

"Edmond with an o," Caro said, pleased with herself for remembering. He bobbed his head at the cops as at a formal introduction, sidled in, taking care not to brush against them. Yet somehow they seemed to be moving in on him. Through the steam, ox-blood eyes swam with distress, looked to Caro for help. She went over. "He's a neighbor," she said and leaned on the open door, smiling the cops out. But at the landing, they had to make way again for the young marrieds. His and Hers, Caro thought of calling out, in case identification were needed. But they were the kind who identified themselves.

"Officer, have you found him?" Hers cried. She clutched at the young one, Caro noticed. His called down the stairwell after them. "We just ate at Joe's Fish House and we looked both coming and going, he's nowhere around there."

His was carrying something too, a glass pitcher with a glass stirring rod, full to the brim with the clear gelid sloosh of martinis. Mustn't *bruise* the gin. That was her father, when she once stirred a batch with a silver spoon.

"Hope you didn't think we weren't coming," His apologized, "we had to go out to eat. She hasn't cooked a meal since we were married."

"All that club aluminum they gave us," Hers said and laughed admiringly at herself.

"Personally," said Edmond, "I think a hot drink is more appropriate on a night like this." Caro wavered between hot and cold: did he mean the weather or the circumstances? "Glug," Edmond said, and Caro saw him in a cartoon drowning. "You know, dear, that Swedish drink, mulled wine with all sorts of goody spices—I have the authentic recipe, not the one in the *Times.*"

Caro said to one and all, come in, come in, but they were already in so she tried to think of something else. "You're sweet, real sweet." She waved her hands helplessly, meaning that all she could offer, with cops buzzing in and out, was a half-gallon jug of California white wine the Morrises had left under the sink, not to be confused with the bottle of Clorox. Herself, she didn't drink. She always said that modestly, hoping to hurt no one's feelings. It took her another moment to think of glasses, but Mrs. Dana had already started washing the ones in the sink. "Oh, that's enough, Mrs. Dana," she protested, "I don't touch the stuff myself."

"That's nice," Mrs. Dana said but she finished them all, scrubbed out the sink. "I think I'll have just a taste of that hot wine, then I'll run along, you've got company enough."

Don't go, don't go, everyone cried, Caro loudest of all.

"We're all going to stay here," Hers declared, chin jutting with determination, "until they find him. It's the least we can do."

His started to pour her a glass of wine, but Edmond pushed him away and demonstrated that pouring a hot liquid into a glass required expertise. And first a spoon in the glass. "Or it will break," he pointed out caustically. But finding it too hot to hold, Mrs. Dana poured it out into a cup. His raised an eyebrow meaningfully at Hers, who acknowledged receipt with a raised one of her own and asked, sweetie, for a martini. Restored to bonhomie, His told Caro that Dorothy was coming too. "She sent her boy friend out to the delicatessen, and she's bringing up sandwiches for them as hasn't eaten as soon as he gets back."

Caro stared, waiting for what came next. Edmond laughed, His looked embarrassed. "You did ask her too, didn't you?"

Caro's smile was blank.

"The nightingale in 1-A, Florence, that is."

"What do you know, Mrs. Dana?" Caro called to her, "we're having a party."

"That's nice," Mrs. Dana said, but absentmindedly, as to kids not fighting.

"George is not back yet."

Caro turned her smile on Edmond. He would now tell her who George was.

"I really don't know what's keeping him, he hasn't called or anything—maybe I should leave him a note telling him to come up."

Caro kept smiling, waiting for him to tell her who George was, but Edmond turned pettishly away. "No, I won't. Let him wonder where *I* am for a change. He'll be sorry he missed all the excitement."

From the window, Hers beckoned them over. "The place is really crawling with cops." Kneeling on the windowseat they all looked out. His and Hers coupled together, arms around each other. Hers said, "What are they doing? Going into every house?"

Mrs. Dana filled her cup again, muttering something no one heard.

"Oh, won't George be mad." Edmond made himself comfortable with a mound of pillows. "Yuk," he said, "what's this?"

Caro held out her hands and took the dried crusts of peanutbutter sandwiches that had been knocked off the sill. Cupped in my palms, she thought, all his mortal remains. Tenderly she carried them to the door, answering the bell.

The nurse, no dyke she, bore breast-high a tray before her. She held it out, neighborly offering to Caro, who nodded and smiled and said Dorothy to show she knew the name, but did not extend her hands. Hers came over to admire all the pretty shapes. "You ought to go in for catering, Dorothy," she said and put the tray down on the dropleaf. Relieved, Caro deposited the crusts on it. His was quick to pour out a martini. Edmond asked after the boy friend. Dorothy sat down like a woman glad to be off her feet, stuck her legs straight out in front of her. Caro gritted her teeth, it was like the scrape of chalk on blackboard to see a woman sit like that, making of her legs slick nylon-glazed obstacles to trip over.

"He's talking to the cops over on Montague. He thinks he saw some kids playing in the construction site over there—swiping things probably—" She looked over at Caro and became suddenly the nurse on duty. Eat, she ordered. Eat, the others echoed the order. Caro obeyed, picking without looking. Nibbled away on dried crusts.

Caro forced herself to look away from Dorothy's legs, to look at Hers. Hers was sitting on one, but swinging the other. She wore boots, soft crushed leather that came over the knee. Yet she could move the joint. "That's pretty good," Caro said, smiling in frank admiration at the swinging of the leg.

Dorothy patted her on the back. "That's the girl," she said. Hers looked over with some disdain. At her? Caro wondered. But it was at the room. Hers was making herself cozy with criticism. "The Morrises didn't do much with this place, did they?" Caro smiled amiably. There should be music. Someone should put on a record. You couldn't have a party without music.

"Where's Mrs. Dana?"

Soft fuzzy dream took on the cold clear precision of a nightmare.

"Where's Mrs. Dana?" Caro demanded.

No one knew. She was there a moment ago. Now she was gone. No one had seen her leave. Caro stared over their heads through the closed windows into another room equally empty.

Dorothy said she heard something, from outside. Caro stared down at the Magnavox, trying to remember what she had been going to do. The kid's name, muted by a great distance and many years of time, rang in her ears, as if someone there in the room had just pronounced it. Once just outside Delhi, when they were picnicking along some canal, sitting on the hot sand and cooling their feet in the water, she had heard her father call her. Caro. She had heard it. But he's dead, Sidney pointed out. I don't care, Caro said, rubbing her thin upper arms as if they were cold, I heard it.

There were Puerto Ricans up the block, His said. His and Hers admired them. Their joie de vivre accounted for almost anything you heard outside, from crashing bottles to Latin crooners.

Edmond screeched. "No, something is going on down there."

A window was flung open. His and Hers looked out over Edmond's shoulder. Dorothy ran over. Caro stood back, feeling the cold air hit her face with such force she was sure she couldn't breathe. You can drown in air, she thought. It was a discovery.

"It's the kid! They've found him!"

"Whaddya mean *they*. That's Mrs. Dana coming down the street with him."

Trust Mrs. Dana.

"What are they all huddled there in the middle of the street for?"

"The kid's all right, you can tell that."

Caro turned from speaker to speaker, listening to the reports. Someone called up: This the kid all right? She was pulled to the window. Leaned out, looked below. Mrs. Dana had the kid by one hand; with the other she brushed back his hair, tilted his head up. There must have been five, six cops, and two police cars, their red lights blinking. She leaned further out, giggling: this was a room, a window, a time and place for throwing kisses down to strange men. Edmond, made nervous, grasped her by the waist, then seeing a car park, let her go so suddenly she almost fell out. "That's George," he cried and pushed his own head through. "George!" he yelled, "George, I'm up here."

There was a rush for the door. An exodus into the hall. They gathered at the top of the stairs, listening to the ascent of young hand in hand with old, and strangely matching in pace. Only Caro stayed behind. Ravenously hungry, she took up her station by the sandwiches, leaned against the dropleaf, heard it groan. With the surreptitious quickness of the guilty about to be caught, she moved the tray to the other table, polished off the dropleaf with the raised hem of her skirt. She heard the questions rained down, where what how when, the old woman's answer bleated up: "Just like I said, he was at a friend's. Watching TV. No sense of time." The sandwiches were so little, she stuffed in two at a time.

There he was, carried in like the hero of a ball game on the shoulders of a victory-flushed crowd. Only, she had to admit, he didn't look like what he had won amounted to much. She swallowed with a grimace, somewhere there had been fish paste and she didn't like fish paste.

"So you did make a friend," she said, and because he was still holding Mrs. Dana's hand, added somewhat maliciously, "Like I said."

"I'm sorry," the kid said, but she could not tell, staring at his face, if he was. In a fit of annoyance she ripped off her lashes. They stuck to her fingers, sticky as caterpillars. At a loss where to put them, she had an inspiration, stuck them upside down on her forehead above the line of her brows. The kid laughed. She could see him more clearly now.

"What's to be sorry?" she agreed.

"Vito, I mean." He was solemn—sorry again. "Mrs. Dana says you were worried, you didn't get to go."

"Vito? Who he?" She had really forgotten about Vito. And vice versa. The creep hadn't even called. It couldn't matter less whether she came or not. Well, fuck him, or rather, she corrected herself neatly as a newscaster, let someone else. But still, all the pleasant smooth-flowing slow-tempo fuzziness of the evening was gone. She gnawed at a hangnail, moved jerkily toward him, got a hold of his shoulder, gave him a little push away for a scold, a pull toward for love. Added together, that made one shake before she lost altogether the feel of him under the slippery padded nylon of his jacket.

"You've lost your schoolbag."

She found out that if she looked straight through, not at, his glasses, she could see his eyes quite clearly. They were round and dark and astonished wide, with an orphan-look of bereavement as he realized his loss.

"That's all right, I'll get you another one." Leaning over to unzip him, she gave him the kiss they were all waiting for. Everybody let loose, as if that had been the stroke of twelve on New Year's Eve. How, they wanted to know, talking and laughing at once, how in the world, Mrs. Dana, did you find him? Mrs. Dana smiled, inscrutably oriental behind the maquillage of her wrinkles.

"I think I'll have another drop of that hot wine," she said, and with her eyes squirrel-bright, enjoying her secret, she smacked her lips over the aromatic brew, making them ask how how how all over again before she gave in and told them.

"I called him. That's all. I called him." She sat down, spread her lap, opened her coat and began to laugh. "Those poor cops, going up and down all those stairs, knocking on all those doors. It would take them till kingdom come. Now in my day, a kid didn't come home to supper, his ma stuck her head out the window and yelled. The best place to yell here is out back in the courtyard. All the buildings this block, the next, have their rear ends opening on to that courtyard. So I went out there and just yelled." But she wasn't giving everything away, her wink and nod and smirk told them that as she sipped at her drink. "Course there's an art to child-calling, though I say it myself as shouldn't."

They weren't letting her hold anything back. Show us, Mrs. Dana, show us how you do it. Well, she agreed, and put down her drink, and slapped the arms of her chair and stood up, spreading her legs apart, raising her hands to cup her mouth, throwing her head back. But first: a few final words of instruction.

"You gotta call loud of course and clear, but there's more to it than that. You gotta call like you *mean* it, and you gotta call like you *know* they can hear. That's what they're all going to say, you know, if you don't call right: I didn't *hear* you, ma."

Resuming the correct position, she called out the kid's name, high old voice but piercingly loud, making the windowpanes rattle, mounting to a crescendo on the first syllable, plateauing out on the second, carrying through all the rooms and out the windows and down the street, calling demanding insisting identifying caller and called, the sound roping its way through the foreign territories of the night, lingering at the end, stretching, hovering, tautening to a noose, pulling tight, pulling back, back home.

It was the most beautiful sound Caro had ever heard. Shoulders hunched, hair in her face, sucking on her own blood, she began to cry, but noiselessly, holding her breath not to shorten by an instant the lingering echo of that beautiful cry. Beautiful, beautiful. If someone had called her like that, she'd have come. She left it to the others to surround the old woman, laughing, cheering, slapping her on the back to help her recover from the paroxysm of coughing which followed the expenditure of so much breath. Caro stayed quite still, hearing long after the dissolution of the cry, through all the party's continuing noise, the kid's name called.

Give Brother My Best

I hate family affairs. I have come back from this last one irritable, depressed. The wedding of a daughter of a cousin of my husband's mother—I had to laugh. You call that a family, I asked my husband on the way back, this monstrous aggregate, inflated to gargantuan size with uncles, aunts, cousins, in-laws, whose vociferous greetings will be followed by complete silence until the next occasion. An occasional family. No wedding, anniversary, birth, funeral occurs but kinship is reasserted like a ritual oath. They convoke like the annual congress of a professional society, whose members have no personal ties, nothing in common beyond the shop talk of their kinsman trade.

Even to his brother and sister my husband is polite, presents what I recognize as his company face, as if they had never lived together in one house where doors slammed with hate, wills clashed in hot kitchens, cold beds were for plotting, sides were taken at the dining table, and jokes exploded like fireworks, shattering faces with laughter.

We were a *real* family—Brother and Sister, Mama and Daddy—marked like cards in an Old Maid deck, answering to no other name. Flesh and blood. Flesh and blood. That was Mama's call to arms. That was the family. Yet it was more than that: it was her hard stony virgin plot carved out of the wilderness of the world. She had seeded it, weeded it, nourished it, guarded it: within its confines her flesh and blood would grow, flourish, multiply—who knows what homey touch of megalomania distinguished her dreams? Meanwhile, to

Brother and me, the thought of ever living beyond that tightly defined territory was as fantastic as the exploration of outer space.

Before the front door of our house we shed neighbors and school friends, even Daddy his business cronies, as meticulously as if we were Japanese removing our shoes soiled with the outdoors. When guests did penetrate into the living room, the barricades were not dismantled, only drawn back a few yards to the corridor of bedroom doors, firmly closed. No one ever dropped in. The rare visitors were heralded far in advance, and then Mama's hospitality was magnificent. Cake was baked, ice cream cranked in the freezer on the back porch, the good china and crystal brought down from the top of the kitchen cupboard to gleam more conspicuously on open shelves. Curtains were washed and ironed, and the faded cretonne slipcovers removed from the sofa to display the maroon plush upholstery, bought in the prosperous twenties but now afflicted with bald patches of worn nap like an elegant disease of the rich. So two chivalric armies might meet on a field of gold: the glitter of raiment and trappings, the mouthing of politenesses, the formal alignment of forces (Mama always in a straight-back chair moved in from the dining room, facing her guests, never sitting along side of them)—all this was but the daily warfare continued in a minor mode.

The war was all in Mama's mind, but to us she projected her hallucinations with greater force than reality could muster. She was a Northerner buried in the deep South, a Lutheran awash in Baptist waters, a stranger with no blood kin within a thousand miles. Daddy, if allowed, would have defected to the enemy long ago— poor Daddy with his cocker spaniel soul—but Mama played grim watchdog over us all.

Even Brother and I, hating each other as only close kin do, felt joined together in our differences from all others. Come in and see my dolls, a school friend would say, swinging on her screen door until someone inside ordered her to close it to keep the flies out. Hesitantly I would enter—knowing no such invitation could come from me—walk through the dark front hall on timid tiptoe, like a wild animal scenting some trap, not touching anything, not even the handle of a door, letting it be opened for me, making my friend walk through first, and, again like an animal, most terrified because the very smell of her house was different from the smell of ours.

To this day, I don't know what was different about the smell. Our floors were scrubbed with the same harsh yellow Octagon soap, our clothes boiled in the same black pots over the same wood fires, and for the most part we ate the same food. Mama's cooking had slid imperceptibly into the Southern idiom of deep-fat frying, cream sauces, hot biscuits, and cornbread. Perhaps twice a year, as if militantly reaffirming her Pennsylvania origins, she made her own scrapple and baked a shoo-fly pie, which, without liking overmuch, we accepted on the table solemnly, like the bitter herbs of a Jewish seder.

Our frequent moves from one neighborhood to another, followed the exigencies of Daddy's disastrous business career. With each bankruptcy came ignominious removal: Mama more proud, we more shy, the family more close-knit. Only Daddy remained incorrigible, both in winning friends and losing money—linked in Mama's mind as cause and effect, further acidulating her misanthropy.

I remember her railing: "Out to lunch, out to lunch —you were out to lunch four hours—four hours by the clock—from the time I first phoned until you finally answered. Customers could be beating on the door, and where are you? Out to lunch!" Mama's virulence lent itself at times to such Swiftean extravagance. None of us, not even she, could really imagine customers beating on the door. And she knew he was not eating, but out somewhere with the "boys," playing cards, fishing, hunting, or perhaps just leaning over a Coke machine swapping jokes. It was, after all, the Great Depression, and lunch or no lunch, his little businesses were no doubt doomed to failure—the gas station, the radio repair shop, the ice cream parlor, the food brokerage where, for several months, he hovered in some nebulous purgatory between wholesale and retail and ended up with three cases of peanut butter which we lived on for weeks.

Nevertheless, this "out to lunch" sign inevitably became a neighborhood joke. It was one of those signs with a painted clock face and two cardboard hands to position at the hour of intended return. When he left at noon, he would set the hands at one, but the slightest jar of the door would cause them to collapse on six-thirty. If the hands did not fall of their own accord, some prankster would see to it.

Bankruptcy always proved Mama's point, and in the bustle of moving, she would bludgeon Daddy with cheerfulness: "At least there's no place to go now but up." When we moved to Beecham Street, however, she said nothing at all.

Beecham Street climbed straight up a hill, and there on the crown was the Federal Penitentiary. Al Capone was housed there. As I remember it, this was our claim to fame, *Gone With the Wind* not yet having been written. The hill had been bare when the prison was built, but now its sides were scored with narrow streets, studded with boxlike frame bungalows, rectangular, monotonous, cheap. Always before, wherever we lived, no matter how old and decrepit and rambling the structure—even if a flat of rooms over a store—we could find just down the block, sometimes next door, a fine house, at least some substantial ones. Street addresses gave nothing away: our income, our social position were shaded under a leafy ambiguity. But Beecham Street was the first of those new "developments"—presaging the low-income housing projects yet to come—of houses built at the same time by the same contractor to the same plan for the same people. Poor people. A little mill town without a mill. Although, now that I think of it, the Pen could have passed for one. Many old factories had the same fierce brick castellated air.

No need here for shrieking chalk reminders of the wages of sin or the imminent approach of the kingdom of heaven. At night the searchlights playing over the prison yard rhythmically swooped across bedroom windows, and in the dark the sleepers shuddered as if diddled by the finger of God. No longer was "the Boogie-man'll get you if you don't watch out," childhood's cautionary refrain. Instead, "you'll wind up in the Pen some day," we were promised. The Boogie-man we could outgrow, but the Pen was always there and we didn't have far to go. Like the fine steady settling of soot from the prison chimneys, rectitude rained on us.

Mama settled herself in this new house, shivering like the emperor who for the first time felt the nakedness of his fine clothes. It was then I am sure she gave up on Daddy. It was then she must have turned to Brother as the great white hope of the family.

Remembering Brother as he was then, I can see why. That was the summer of—'36, '37?—somewhere around there. He was to enter high school in the fall with straight A's behind him. I suppose that even as a child he was unusually attractive—what big eyes you have, people were always telling him (my eyes were just as big, but no one ever said so). And that summer something happened to him that even I could see—it was like the brightness of a star exploding into the blinding blaze of a supernova, so that Mama's eyes, when she looked at him, watered like the eyes of someone who has stared too long at the sun. His voice had changed without cracking, his good looks hung on the edge of manliness without once stumbling into pimples and gawkiness. Girls were crazy about him, older girls—he was tall for his age—but it was more than that. Even grown-ups clustered around him like flies after honey. Mama was proud of his good manners. He spoke up with assurance, never squirmed or fidgeted, and always remembered to say sir or ma'am. Only Daddy found something to be displeased about, but just what he couldn't put his finger on. Smart-alecky, was the term he finally settled for.

"Smart-alecky," he complained to Mama, "did you hear him with Ben Chalmers? A man like that." That was right after the junior high graduation, when Mr.

Chalmers had made a speech and given out prizes, two of them to Brother. Mr. Chalmers was something big in the Junior Chamber of Commerce and also something big in a charitable organization that devoted its good works to fatherless boys. After the exercises, he took Brother aside to congratulate him, returned him to Mama and Daddy with words of warm praise. He was a big moon-faced man, with a button nose and the rimless glasses that were considered most becoming in those days—the first man I ever smelled, not counting sweat. It must have been a scented shaving lotion. That and the French cuffs on his shirt sleeves placed him in a class far above us.

"You don't know what you're talking about," Mama refuted Daddy bluntly, for Mr. Chalmers had offered Brother a part-time summer job, which showed what a good impression Brother had made. And it was she who insisted that Brother accept, called him lazy—"just like your father"—when he hesitated.

"I know you," she scolded him fondly, "you want to spend all summer in the swimming pool, like last year, but you're old enough now, Brother, to begin thinking about your future. It's good Christian work, too, helping Mr. Chalmers on outings for those poor little boys, it'll do you no harm to learn that there are others less fortunate than you."

The only time I remember Mama ever admitting that. Her platform for life called for never looking down, only up. It was Daddy who pointed out the cripples and told us, with the serene complacent cheerfulness of a man who has left his children well provided for, to thank God we had two arms and two legs. Mama, on the other hand, directed our Sunday afternoon rides—the current price wars among the gas stations made this the cheapest entertainment—to the most exclusive residential areas of the city, where fabulous estates could be glimpsed behind fortresslike walls. She had a cheerfulness of her own in pointing out to us, whenever a rise in the ground or a turn in the road permitted, a spot of Gothic tower or a ripple of red Spanish tile, as if all this grandeur was our inheritance from *her,* once a few legal formalities were gone through.

Brother at least seemed to get the message, and that summer began the ascent. Effortlessly. That was the crux of the matter. Without any effort at all. What the vigor of Mama's imagination had seen as a great sword-clashing battle, calling for rigorous training, adventurous daring, persistent attack—for which she had forged the virtue of the family's ways, the purity of its vision, the strength of its cohesion, the truth of its being—Brother promised to achieve with just his blue eyes. And his blond hair combed into a high wave. As effortlessly as his brown arms swooped up and cut down to cleave the water.

Mr. Chalmers had taken him under his wing, and his patronage promised more for the future than a part-time summer job. Mama and Daddy whispered together about college scholarships or even a West Point appointment, for which Mr. Chalmers had the necessary congressman in his pocket. Daddy was particularly pleased with that congressman. He mentioned him often, hands in his own pocket, jingling coins in vicarious affluence. The afternoon I caught Brother at a city swimming pool when he was supposed to be on the job—and of course told on him—Mama had a fit. Didn't Brother realize the importance of making good on this summer job? Didn't he know what depended on it? What, she demanded of him, would Mr. Chalmers think if he played hookey like that?

He's really caught it this time, I thought with some satisfaction, but Brother just slapped his wet towel and suit over the back porch railing, poured a cold drink from the ice box, combed his still-damp hair in the hall mirror—Mama ever on his heels eloquent with prophecies of disaster—picked up the tightly rolled afternoon paper on the front porch and began to read the funnies. Desperate, she tore it out of his hands and swatted him with it. He looked at her with the same sulky air of forbearance he assumed when she nagged him about homework or criticized his friends.

"Did you at least call the man and tell him you were sick?" she pleaded.

"Yes," Brother said, eyeing the funnies, "I called him."

Mama sighed in defeat and gave him back the paper.

"Well I hope nobody else saw you at the pool. These things get around you know."

Brother snickered, already deep in the funnies. But because she continued to stand over him in a gloom of worry, he threw her a reassurance. "You're getting upset over nothing, Mama, it's not that kind of a job. I can do pretty much what I please, that's the way Mr. Chalmers wants it."

Mama didn't believe that. To her there was only one kind of a job: you worked hard, you applied yourself, you made good. But she had to admit that Brother's way seemed the way Mr. Chalmers wanted it. Brother not only kept the job but was granted guest privileges at Mr. Chalmers's country club, where he could practice swimming in an Olympic-sized pool and mingle with the wealthy on terms that to us at home, overhearing telephone calls, were frighteningly chummy.

Whatever kind of a job it was, Brother continued to have plenty of time for swimming. At the midsummer swim meet, he turned out to be the star. That boy should be trained for the Olympics, was what Daddy overheard.

Mama and I missed that—at the last moment I had vomited, been put to bed, and Daddy had driven off alone with Brother. It must have been a great night— the outdoor pool in Grant Park especially lit up, temporary bleachers for the city notables, a big shirt-sleeved crowd sucked to the water's edge by the black-velvet summer heat. As a swimmer Brother was good, but it was on the high dive that he leaped into greatness. I know very well how he walked out on the board, gave it a few little test springs, stood there with his arms upraised, motionless, the muscles of his stomach taut, manufacturing drama in the stillness and the silence, as if a drum were rolling. Poor Mama, she had to wait until they got back to hear all about it, and I woke up too, fully recovered, to listen to Daddy's midnight account of glory.

For me that became the great occasion—being up in the middle of the night, with darkened houses all around us, but our light still burning—the neighbors blotted out by sleep and we alone, a small tight conclave of life huddled together around the kitchen table, under the protecting circle of the harsh overhead light. This was the family, I saw it so for the first time, though I know now this is the way Mama always saw it. I could even see the kinship of our faces, faces that before had been unique. Mine would grow long and elastic, drooping unaware into ludicrous moues like Daddy's, while Brother's shared the broad-browed, blunt-nosed handsomeness of Mama's. Only his had a fleshiness, packed firmly (for he was so young) around his wide nostrils, rounding his cheeks, filling out his lips, that I doubt hers had ever known. Certainly as I remember hers, it had squared off against the world into granite hardness, only her eyes—hazel, not blue—small, retiring under the bony ridge, still soft and uncongealed.

"He came over and introduced himself—he's a friend of Ben Chalmers—it seems Ben's been bragging about you, Brother—and said that boy of yours sure can dive, and I said, well, he's not bad for his age, and he said, not bad? why that boy'll be state champion before he graduates, you mark my words, he ought to start training right now for the Olympics—that's what he said, Brother—and then he just up and asked me to come on out to his plant and pick me a bushel of peaches before they're all gone—free, I made sure of that, Mama—and bring your boy too, he said, he can have all he can eat."

Mr. Haskell. I remember his name, but not much else about him. Just another notch on Brother's gun belt, I thought that night. A strange lady stops me on the street. I smirk, at last I am noticed, admired. But she asks, is that your brother, child? I had my own fantasies: Shirley Temple surrounded by the Damon Runyon crowd, Merrylips among the cavaliers. Only to Brother it happened in real life, like this—the invitation to all the peaches he could eat.

Daddy had fantasies of his own, Brother's success having gone to his head. "Your Mr. Chalmers had better watch out," he said, nudging Brother, "I think Mr. Haskell aims to steal you away from him. Asked me if you needed a part-time job. Says he's got one open in his town office that pays real good. You find out how much, Brother, then we'll see." His laugh embraced and swallowed up Brother. "We'll see, yessir, we'll see," he repeated, as if it were the punch line of a joke.

We drove out the next day, in spite of Mama's warning: "I hope you know what you're doing. Chances are he won't know you from Adam, so you'd better be ready to pay for them."

The peaches I remember. The smell of them bruised, in bushel baskets piled high outside the corrugated tin of the packing plant. The white heat of midafternoon in a hot July. Flies thick as dust flurries, carousing in the odiferous air. Peaches purpled, sunken-cheeked, skinned raw in spots, stinking sweet. I can feel my mouth pucker over the fuzz of the peel before my teeth bite through into the juicy flesh.

Only Daddy and Brother went into the shed. I unstuck my sweaty behind from the seat to follow, but Mama grabbed hold of my skirt and pulled me back. Miss Tagalong, she called me on such occasions. "You just climb right back in the car, Miss Tagalong. That's no place for a child." Or for a girl. If it wasn't one, it was the other—life was one enormous plot to get me out of the way. I suppose I howled, because Mama turned around in her seat and swung her purse at me. It missed by a mile. It always did the first time, just as the second time it would land hard, smack along the cheek. Her purse was of black leather, supple and worn, fat cheeks bulging, and with it Mama swung all the weight and authority of the household. It held her department store bills, with itemized sales slips. It held letters from her distant relatives and empty envelopes she was saving for the return address. It held her three bankbooks —she never trusted any one bank again, not after they had closed down on her in '33, but parceled out her small savings among several. It held shopping lists and receipts for gas and light and water. It was her safe, her office file, her household ledger. It was as sanctified a symbol of power as the Roman lictor's bundle of rods with the embedded axe, and after it swished once threateningly over my head, I sprawled submissive for the moment in the back seat.

Someone appeared at the entrance of the shed, a tall man in a wilted seersucker suit. Mr. Haskell? Daddy took off his panama and wiped the top of his head apologetically, like a man asking for directions. The man laughed and shook Daddy's hand, and then put his hand on Brother's head, rubbing it playfully. They went inside, into the cool-seeming darkness, with the man's arm thrown over Daddy's shoulders. Just before he vanished, I saw Brother reaching into his hip pocket for his comb.

"Hot as an oven," Mama complained, "they'd better not be long."

Everything is still in that white heat. The noise from the packing plant reaches us as a soft soporific hum. The faintest threads of white cloud in the sky, as if there the faded blue canvas was wearing thin. In the tall sedge grass, not one stalk stirring, the busyness of insects mounts in a buzz, drone, chirrup, crackle. Mama's head nods, her eyes close, I wait for the definitive snore.

It came at last, a beautiful musical sound, like the whistle of a peanut vender's machine. And I was out the window, scuffing my bare feet in the thick dust.

The walls of the shed were fringed with weeds, bone-dry, heat-yellowed, which cracked loudly as I sidled through them. At first I peered cautiously through the open door, lest Daddy see me and send me back, and then sneaked through, to glue my backbone to the inside wall, the way we practiced good posture in p.t. class. It made me feel flatter, more nearly invisible. In the center of the shed, throughout its length, women were paddling their arms in a trough of peaches, a wrist flicking here and there, removing a discard, sizing, grading, intent as miners panning gold. Around them moved bare-torsoed men, shouldering the baskets in and out, loading them on flat trolleys. No seersucker suit to be seen anywhere. I finally located Daddy over by a Coke machine at the far end of the shed, drinking and talking and laughing with two men, foremen, no doubt, for they wore shirts. He had his jacket folded over his arm, and he was leaning against the machine with his thumb hooked over his belt, and I could tell he wasn't going any place soon. He always looked different to me when I saw him like that, away from us, among strangers.

For one thing, he didn't look at all like the "married man with two children to feed," which was Mama's reiterated definition of him. There he slouched, long-limbed and thin and as gawky with his height as if he had just shot up over the summer and wasn't used to it yet, his tight round pot-belly no more than a sofa pillow tucked in a boy's shirt. And when he had finished his joke and one of the other men had started on his, I saw how he listened, his long face poised on the starting-line of laughter, his two big front teeth, with the childlike gap between them, biting down over his underlip in delight. Whereas at home, playing father of two children with insatiable appetites, he rounded his shoulders and pulled down the lines of his face, and didn't say much, and when he looked at us, his glance skittered nervously away, as if—eye to eye—we might catch on he was just pretending to great worries, to please Mama.

Of course, it was that utter inability to appreciate disaster that drove Mama wild, but to me, a child, to whom only fun and play was real too, he seemed wholly wonderful then. That afternoon in the packing shed I hated and envied Brother as never before, seeing that Daddy could look like that when they went off together, but never at home with me.

I had not noticed until then that Brother wasn't there. I looked all over, but he wasn't in the shed at all. Nor, I remembered, was the seersucker suit. One of the workmen approached the Coca Cola machine, hiking up his khaki pants in shy subservience before he spoke to the shirted men, much as in another age he would have tugged at a forelock and bent a knee. One of them looked out over the heads of the workers and called, "Mr. Haskell." You could tell that was the name of the boss: all the noise stopped, the rattle of trolleys ceased, people stood still and looked up and around and at each other. There was no answer. With all those eyes searching him out, I could not hope to stand there unseen. I inched my way back to the door and out into the blinding brightness.

Wherever Brother was, he was with Mr. Haskell. I pictured him gorging on peaches, all he could eat. I would have all I could eat too, when Daddy finally carted the bushel basket to the car, but it wasn't the same. I wanted to be hand-fed, like Brother, by someone who smiled down on me the way the man in the seersucker suit had smiled down on him, a two-way smile that asked as much as it gave. Stubborn on the scent, I skirted the side of the building, where the trucks were drawn up, and rounded it to the back. There was nothing there but broken crates and baskets, some enormous garbage cans, and the kind of little junk pile of rubber tires, empty oil cans, rusty bits of machinery, that every plant drops like excrement at its rear. Beyond the wide field of sedge grass, matted down by the criss-crossing of innumerable tracks, the orchard took over, precisely marching to the horizon. I almost missed them. A few more steps and they would have seen me before I saw them, standing in the shade of the single stray peach tree that grew almost next to the shed, as if one long summer ago somebody had happened to spit out a seed there.

I kept back behind the garbage cans, at a loss for my next move. They were talking but I couldn't hear what they said. Mr. Haskell had his hand on Brother's shoulder. With a playfulness that somehow offended me to see in a grown-up man, he reached inside Brother's shirt and tickled his back, offending Brother too, apparently, for he squirmed away and started back to the shed. I crouched lower and no longer peered around the can, but I could hear them now. I heard Mr. Haskell's voice, deep, unctious, bent on pleasing, and everything he said began with a chuckle and ended with a laugh, like quotation marks attributing the words in between to someone else. "I'll fix it up with your old man about the game next Saturday—the way I hear it from Ben, you're quite a baseball fan." And I heard Brother reply, politely enough to make Mama proud, "Well, sir, if you want to know the truth, I can take it or leave it—baseball, that is—but I'll take it, so long as I get the five bucks *first.*" Mr. Haskell chuckled deeper, "Don't you trust me, son?" he asked, and laughed louder, and Brother said, "Oh, yes sir, it would sort of spoil things if I couldn't. Sir." Even I could hear the insolence seeping through that last belated title of respect, but Mr. Haskell just chuckled and laughed again, but with nothing in between this time.

They re-entered the shed, and I made a dash for the car, my only concern at the moment to be safely sprawled on the back seat when Mama woke up. Only with her head again lolling heavily in front of me, did I consider the significance of what I had heard. That Mr. Haskell should not only take Brother to a ball game, but pay for the privilege. Farewell o Shirley Temple and goodbye Merrylips—inept fantasies dissolved once and for all in the acid bath of reality, that clear view, snatched from behind a garbage can, of the supreme potency of Brother's charm.

They came back soon with the bushel of peaches, and Mama woke up and examined the basket critically. "How much did you pay for them," she asked suspiciously, when she couldn't find any rotten ones, even underneath.

"They were free, I tell you," Daddy said, wearing again his worried "family-man" face. "Brother made a hit with Mr. Haskell all right. He's taking him to the ball game Saturday," he added quickly, probably to soften her up, and she was pleased and good-humored all the way home.

It was months later—no longer the baseball but the football season—before I found out no one else knew about the money. By then it had become a ritual on Sunday morning for Brother to turn over to Mama his weekly part-time earnings. Before she held out her hands, she wiped them on her apron, and he prolonged the show by carefully unrolling and smoothing out the crumpled wadded-up bills, and stacking the coins in neat piles. And she counted it out all over again, impressing us with the magnificent total—ten, sometimes fifteen dollars—her fingers spinning the coins from the table into her palm with a storekeeper's computer speed. Although the summer job was over, he seemed to be making just as much from the caddying he did at the country club. Some of the loose change was always returned to him for pocket-money—more than Daddy thought good for him I have no doubt, there was something sly about the way Mama folded up Brother's fingers around the coins, sealing his fist with a fond tap.

His birthday fell on a Sunday that year, and on that occasion Mama enclosed a green bill in his hand. Even Brother was amazed when he saw that it was a five, not a single. The next day he spent it all on a wallet, a genuine leather one, more than that, a leather we had never seen before—tough as pigskin but the grain pocked with little puckered circles like embroidered eyelets. Ostrich, he told us, and we were certainly awed. Five dollars for a wallet—five dollars! That was enough for a week's groceries, if you were careful to buy the specials. Mama had to fight back her tears, but Daddy laughed so loud, in a woman it would have sounded hysterical. It became one of his pet stories about Brother, that fine ostrich wallet. "All his money for a wallet, and nothing left to put in it!"

It was the wallet that gave him away. Mama had come into the bathroom to clean up after Brother's bath —she always complained about having to do that, but still she did it. There, with his dirty sneakers, wet towel, underwear, she had found the ostrich-skin wallet. She called him, all set to hand it over after the usual lecture about his untidiness and carelessness—"money doesn't grow on trees, you know"—when she noticed how thick the wad of green was. He grabbed for it, but she blocked him with that hard square shoulder of hers and counted forty-seven dollars.

She couldn't make a sound. It was Brother's yell that

brought Daddy and me running. When Daddy saw the money, his face reddened in blotches as if he had just been slapped and he croaked, "Even I don't carry around that kind of money."

Of course they were sure he had stolen it. Daddy kept threatening to call the police, but neither Mama nor Brother paid any attention to him. They kept eyeing each other like two crouching wrestlers waiting to get a stranglehold. Mama moved in and tried to pin him against her breast. "You've got to tell us where you got that money, dear," she said. "We'll see that you don't get into trouble, but you've got to tell us the truth."

With all of us crowded into the bathroom, there was hardly room to move, the air was still steamy from Brother's bath, but nobody thought to get out. Brother backed away from Mama, bumped into Daddy. Daddy sat down suddenly on the toilet seat, and stayed there, looking constipated. Mama maneuvered around to get another bear-hug on Brother, but he stiff-armed her away. "You had no right to look in that wallet," he countered, "I didn't steal that money, and as for any-thing else, it's none of your business. For Chrissake, I'm not a snot-nosed kid." (That was aimed at me in the doorway.) I could tell what was coming. Brother would work himself into a rage, the way a girl would break down in tears, to ward off a showdown. "You've got to stop spying on me, you hear. Asking who is it, before you call me to the telephone. Straightening out my bureau drawers—straightening out, I *bet.* Looking into my wallet. You've got to stop it, you'd better leave me alone, you hear."

I didn't intend to say anything. Let him get out of this himself, I thought with tight-lipped satisfaction. I could clear him with one word, just like that, but that word would not come from me. But then I saw Mama crying, tears running down the deep lines beside her nose like water carving canyons in desert rocks.

"He didn't steal it, Mama," I said, "truly he didn't." They all looked at me, but it was Brother's look that held me. He was flushed pink from his bath, his damp hair still held the wave he had set into it, he looked clean and fresh and more handsome than I had ever noticed. But his big blue eyes looked at me and I could see him killing me and coming in to take another bath and looking just as clean and fresh and handsome. When they questioned me, I swore loyally that I just knew Brother wouldn't steal, that was all. Which made Mama pick me up to hug and cry against, choking with endearments.

In the end they had to pretend to believe him—that he had saved it up from his caddying tips. I knew one thing: whatever Brother had done, it was worse than stealing. I didn't want to know more. I stopped spying on him (for the same reason, I suppose, Mama stopped snooping). But it was too late. Without knowing what the crime was, knowing only its enormity, I felt trapped by complicity, gagged by my own guilt.

Every day, walking home from school, I looked up at the Pen on the top of the hill, so conveniently located, just a matter of time. At night, the lights, to which I had long been accustomed, awoke me now, and I would lie still in the darkness, holding my breath until the beam passed my window, passed Brother's window, once more around without yet having discovered where we lay.

I never did tell. I remember evenings that winter when we were all in the living room. I would be sitting at a table, doing homework, and Brother would be sprawled on the floor in front of the radio listening to Gangbusters or some program like that. Daddy would be listening too, but hidden in the old wing-back chair, only the smoke-rings he liked to blow signaling his presence. Mama. Well, Mama would be wearing her reading glasses, poring over the close columns of figures on the stockmarket page, sitting close to the fire to toast her feet, which were always cold. I think she was just beginning then to make cautious little investments against the day when Daddy's next business failed. Every now and then she would look up at us, pushing the glasses onto her forehead, first checking to see if I was working at my lessons, then looking at Brother, love licking at her face as unevenly as the firelight.

It was then I would think about telling. Just think about it. It was like that rock, scissors, paper game that Brother used to play with me, as an excuse for whacking me hard when I lost. Hands behind the back, and at a sign, throw out a fist (rock), or two fingers (scissors), or an open palm (paper). Rock breaks scissors, scissors cuts paper, and paper covers rock. Brother was scissors, mother was rock. If I spoke up (forgetting that scissors would cut me into little bits), paper would cover rock. I played that game over and over in my mind, watching Mama watch Brother, but I never spoke up.

It was to happen almost like that anyway. In his last year of high school, Brother met a pretty Irish girl, from a family Mama at her kindest called "low-down." They were married almost overnight, Brother dropped out of school, got a job as trucker's helper with Railway Express, and had a new baby every year. After that, whenever I saw him, he was drinking beer. He blew up like a balloon, revealing the porcine quality that had always underlain his good looks. In the only snapshot of him I have, taken just before I left home, he looks like a pig. And I think back to how he was a god to Mama, and to me a shining Lucifer, and how he failed us both.

After that, Mama changed. She closed out the family the way Daddy had closed out many a business—cleared the shelves, paid off debts outstanding (when I left home, she cried a little), then locked the doors. I have come back a few times, Brother often, living so near, both alone and with his wife and many children, but the doors don't open. They made a little money during the war—who didn't?—and she plays the stock market. She has a kind of formal camaraderie with her broker and spends her mornings in one of those offices walled in from the street by dark green glass, where the ticker tape is screened. The people sit on seats in rows, get up and walk around, sit again, like passengers in a tight green-walled ship confined to aimlessness while hurling through space toward a far-off but quite definite destination. Afternoons she sleeps, leaving Daddy ambling through the house with a forlorn stoop, the erstwhile "worried family man," now unemployed, like an old vaudeville star who could not make it on the new silver screen.

"*Your* family," my husband snorts. "You and your brother never even write." Which is true. Not for us the pallid middle distance of mere acquaintance. Mama writes—not often, not on any set occasion, when she feels up to it. Her letters are copied studiously like homework. Sometimes, in my belated reply, I add a postscript: How's Brother getting along? And I suppose, calling her, he says, when the conversation flags, "What do you hear from Sister?" And Mama writes, like a disinterested neutral interpreter, weaving back and forth between two hostile states, Brother says to tell you. And I answer, Give Brother my best.

Ariadne

It was as if the knife which had taken out the slack of age had cut away all her sad history as well—the loneliness, the small humiliations that blotched her like a rash, even the insomnia. Sleep came easy again, she no longer had to wrestle each night for it like Jacob struggling with the angel of the Lord. This new face, brought back from the hospital red and swollen as a newborn's, evoked an adoptive tenderness far exceeding that claimed by natural birth. Happiness was its due. All the stories by which her life recounted itself, until now one monotonous tarradiddle of despair, would have a different ending, a happy ending. Beginning with this visit to her sister.

At the suburban bus stop, Lois was waiting, florid and stout, clutching a housewife's heavy handbag and a brown sack of groceries. Without letting go of anything, Lois embraced her, flailing her with the handbag, gathering her in with the groceries. Even as kiss smacked loud on kiss, the quiet computer-clacking of envy had begun. There were the children: two small boys plastered to their mother's side, while Paul, the oldest, in a later stage of mitosis, held himself apart in the rear.

Lois's eyes made their familiar inquisition, last year dreaded, this year staunchly borne, although the new face blushed in shyness, not yet inured to sisterly regard. For relief, she laughed at the shyness of the little ones—the rolling eyes, the lolling tongue, the overall effluvium of mongoloid idiocy emanating from Peter and Reed. Paul was too big now—nine, ten?—to laugh at. He stood aloof, a stranger waiting for another bus, and said, looking in the direction from which it was due, "Hello, Aunt Muff."

Him she loved most of all. She aimed her "Hello, Paul," equally off-side, but she knelt down and kissed the other two all over, lips nuzzling and grazing, suddenly let out to pasture.

"You look good," Lois said grudgingly. And then more pleasantly. "You looked like hell the last time you were here. I suppose for once you took my advice and got some rest."

Ariadne laughed—this year the lines of her face went up, not down—and her eyes were so brilliantly blue, facing as she did the direct rays of the sun, that Lois sank into the depths of depression. She's in love again, she thought. Again.

Even Lois could not tell. Ariadne found it hard to stop laughing, it was so funny, Lois not knowing. Never knowing about the surgeon's hands, large virile hands, manicured into gentleness by success. Your figure is good, he had said, your neckline still holds, it's the face. He had reproached her for the face. (Gray hair effective against Bermuda tan. Older man, after, lately, too many younger ones.) You wear your heart upon your face and of course the face cracks at the seams, he scolded. So she had promised to stop loving. Like promising Daddy to be a good little girl. And he in turn had promised a new face, the old one having been used up.

Just before the knife cut, she sat up in sudden panic, sure that God would punish her for this enormous vanity. Don't draw it up too tight, she pleaded, remembering legendary ladies mysteriously veiled—scarred victims of botched jobs. Sternly he sedated her into abject trust. Trust well-founded. Nothing was too tight. Her new face, like the old, could melt into the soft creases of love, all the little muscles around her eyes and mouth could play out her love. From her hospital bed, she looked at him, felt the inner vibration of her cellular machinery start up again, churning out the sticky secretions of love. Back in his office she said goodbye, but not before she had seen how lost he was behind his desk, lost in the labyrinth of career and marriage and flat photographs of children, how much in need of love to extricate himself from that barren wasteland of successful plastic surgery. Her brows flatly declared her love, but he kept himself barricaded behind his desk and gave careful instructions for her dismissal.

No harm in that. Better than the paralysis which had set in when Alan left. Like the slight tingling pain of blood flowing again in a limb cramped with sleep. A warming-up exercise, nothing serious. She could still laugh, which meant that so far she had kept her promise.

She focused now on Peter and Reed, in summer uniform of brown skin and faded shorts, racing ahead the short blocks home, slapping the pavement rhythmically with thonged sandals. Thin bare legs, knees dark and crusted as tree bark, tender straight toes articulate as fingers. Children. Paul shuffled along beside her—too old to run. Nine? Ten? He was carrying her bag, displaying new manners as last year he had flexed new muscles (but he had not been carrying the bag of groceries, she recalled, enjoying the small triumph).

Lois too noted the bag, its smallness something to be caustic about. "I see you can spare us only the weekend. I suppose we should be grateful for even that."

"Oh, Lois, you sound just like a *relative.*" Ariadne laughed, meaning Lois to laugh with her, as they had laughed together years ago at Aunt Margaret, that relative par excellence—who would first of all remind them how long it had been since their last visit, then complain of the shortness of their present stay, and then demand to know exactly when they planned to come again, counting up their time with her like a bank auditor suspecting them of every intention of absconding— and all before they had yet crossed her threshold.

But Lois did not remember Aunt Margaret. "After all, I *am* your only sister."

After all, I *am* your mother's only sister—Aunt Margaret all over again. They could never answer Aunt Margaret, so they learned to change the subject. She saw the house now, curtains at the attic window. "Did Emory finish the room up there?"

Sighing—though whether from the weight of the groceries or her marriage was not clear—Lois acknowledged the completion of the five-year project. "He put the ceiling up all by himself, some special insulating material, which makes it a little cooler, but not much. I must say he did a good job." Praise squeezed out, like paste from a used-up tube.

Paul was already in the house. The screen door's bang separated them briefly from Peter and Reed. Hoarsely Lois called, "Muff," funneling her sister's nickname into the wide mouth of the paper bag of groceries held to her chest. "I'm glad you're here. Letters are no good—I can't bring myself to write it down. It's Emory. I want to talk to you. Later."

The quick, out-of-the-corner-of-the-mouth whisper, the importunate clutching at a moment's confidence, sent Ariadne speeding up the flagstone walk. "Oh, we'll talk and talk," she promised, and became all girlish flutter and flounce. Even in the sanctuary of the children's presence, she continued to romp and tease and dole out gifts, chattering nonsense, tossing her dark hair, scissored short and straight, as if she still wore the Shirley Temple curls that had always melted her father's heart. Cute as a button, he would weep, and unpack his bags. She had kept them together, being cute as a button, lisping, making her eyes big, bouncing her curls. Mummy loves Daddy? Daddy loves Mummy? Lois had just stood there and watched, arms akimbo, freckles pale, but blue eyes alight with unholy joy.

Peter and Reed had their heads together, furiously whispering in the hall. You do it, no you do it, let's both do it. Together they marched up to Ariadne, faultlessly recited: Little Miss Muffet sat on a tuffet eating her curds and whey. Along came a spider and sat down beside her and frightened Miss Muffet away.

Lois watched them fondly as they turned into spiders. Laughing like a good sport, Ariadne fled, repeating innumerable flights of childhood, teased all the way home from school by boy spiders, while Lois, with red pigtails bouncing and pointed freckled face demurely contained, skipped along the outskirts of the gang, keeping herself carefully unrelated.

Even Paul forgot he was nine years old—ten?—and joined in the chase. It ended with Adiadne trapped at the top of the house, in the new attic room. There on a daybed, covered in practical tweed, she flung herself down in exhaustion, was consumed by spiders. The screams brought Lois plodding up the stairs, to brush the children off her sister, out of the room, with stern admonitions against jumping on the new bed and ruining the springs.

Ariadne stood in the middle of the room, one arm upraised in a wide curve, head twisted downward, like the opening movement of a modern dance. "I heard something tear."

"It's just the seam under the arm, you can fix that," Lois reassured her. "It's your fault, you know, you ask for all that wild stuff. Just like Emory. And then it's up to me to quiet them down." Briskly she straightened the cover of the bed, then sat down, back straight, knees together, in the modesty of middle age which cannot bear any looking up the skirt.

Crouched on the floor by the window—the roof angle made the ceiling too low to stand—Ariadne leaned across the sill and looked down on the street. Children on skate boards. Children on bikes. Children on pogo sticks. In the yard, dashing in and out of sprinklers. A child alone, sitting on the curb, glumly investigating drains.

Lois considered how every joint in her body would creak if she sat that way, considered Ariadne's face, as youthful as that posture, almost the same as when they were young girls rooming together, first adventuring into adulthood. Her own adventure had ended with Emory. Ariadne still labored on. Was it the great romantic quest that kept her young? Or was it no children? As soon as they had spawned, salmon stopped eating, she suddenly remembered from Paul's homework. A wild giggle almost broke the surface, for she had certainly kept on eating. And eating. (As Emory had kept on drinking and drinking.) Yet with the coming of the children, she had stopped so many things: looking in mirrors (really *looking*), waking with expectation, reading fashion ads, taking courses, daydreaming—or night dreaming either, for that matter. She remembered the wild morning rush of getting to work on time—the coffee-brewing, toothbrushing, hair combing, belated skirt pressing—she and Ariadne whirling about their tiny apartment with the speeded up motions of an old Mack Sennett comedy, while she recounted in lavish detail some long exotic dream of the night before. It had been years since she had dreamed a dream like that. Now she fell into bed, pole-axed by fatigue. And the rare dream, when it did come, was always a dull nightmare of some routine gone awry—like not getting the children off to school in time or forgetting to empty the pockets of Emory's no-press work pants before she put them into the washer and finding wads of money—or something else vaguely remembered as of great value—the next morning all sodden and ruined in the suds. Middle-aged dreams. Where was the justice—her heart cried out—that as a child, when it had hurt to be the younger, she had been the younger, but now, when it hurt to be the older, she was lo and behold the older?

"You're mad, aren't you?"

Ariadne refused to speak.

"The funny thing is, I was just trying to please you," Lois said matter-of-factly, as if resigned to forever being misunderstood. "Before you came, I told them to call you Ariadne, that you didn't like to be called Muff, and they were old enough now to pronounce your real name. You know perfectly well they couldn't as babies. So, of course, for the first time they wondered why you were called Muff at all, they could see it wasn't a shortening or anything like that. So I told them. So sue me. I should have made a big mystery of it, I suppose? And they would have thought something awful—you know how kids' minds work—instead of just a sickeningly cute story about you that Daddy made up."

Daddy had never called *her* anything but Lois.

"Oh, Lois," Ariadne expelled her sister's name on

a downward sigh, letting it stand alone as a summing-up. When they had first left home together, she had taken out her real name, donned it with ritual importance, as if it were a jeweled heirloom she had been forbidden to wear until her majority. Then too Lois had tried to please her, conscientiously tried, yet always Muff slipped out, always in front of a new friend.

Lois sulked with her briefly, then, pressed for time, broke the silence. "How do you like the room?"

Ariadne thought of another old joke she and Lois had shared, back when their girl friends had started having babies and demanding compliments. Just for the fun of it, like solving a textbook problem, they spent a whole evening giggling in bed over responses that were both tactful and true. They hit on one meticulously accurate, suitable for all occasions. Now that's what I call a *baby!* they exclaimed from that time on. She could not resist it now.

"Now this is what I call a room!" she said, looking about her admiringly at the amateurishly uneven seams, the lumpy floor tiles, the acoustical ceiling that reminded her of egg cartons. But, from the rawburn redness of Lois's face, she knew that this, unlike Aunt Margaret, had not been forgotten. Frightened by the anger she had evoked—Lois had always been the deadlier fighter—she fingered her new face nervously. In any case, she told herself, praise would have been a tactical error. Lois would have disgorged at once the complaints about Emory so obviously stuck in her craw. You think he's so wonderful, she would have said, and given that bitter laugh like the hawk of phlegm, well, let me tell you. . . .

As it was, she had to defend him. "The trouble with you, Ariadne—" she pronounced the name with distinctness—"you've been going around with playboys so long—excuse me, that shows how old I am, I suppose—it's the jet set now, isn't it?—you have no idea what it's like when a man works for a living. Being manager of a supermarket is no part-time job, let me tell you, and Emory is dog-tired when he gets home. Whatever he does is more than most men do, and is good enough for *me*, thank you."

Lois got up from the couch, a woman with children and much to do, a tight-lipped, straight-backed figure of marital rectitude. In catatonic silence, Ariadne watched her leave the room, shocked at how little Lois knew about her now. Perhaps, way back, when she and Lois had roomed together, there had been a "playboy" or two—she couldn't remember—but long ago she had settled into affairs of impecunious domesticity with lovers young and unestablished. She who yearned to give them everything, to turn herself inside out and spill herself into their hands and was ever being denied the right—only if you were married could you do that— could at least save them money. She fixed up their dark grimy bachelor rooms, made them slipcovers and drapes, cooked in, snapped up shirts whenever she saw them on sale (almost her first question after intimacy was established being neck size and sleeve length), stuck close to neighborhood movies for entertainment, and paid her own way if they were able to arrange vacations together. Yet still Lois pictured her joyriding, nightclubbing, theater-partying. As if, marrying Emory and departing, she had taken all existence with her, leaving Ariadne behind with the debris of moving, an unchanging fixture of the past. As if there was nothing to her sister but what was mired in her memory of their girlhood together.

Trailing Lois down to the kitchen, Ariadne saw their mother in that broad swayed back, the denim wraparound skirt tied around it much as the apron had been around their mother's. And in the kitchen, Lois lorded it much as their mother had done in hers, refusing all help, intolerant of any other way of doing things, unable to bear a pot or ladle or a dish put back in the wrong place. It was an act of charity for Lois to let her scrape the carrots.

"Cut them into very thin strips," Lois said, "otherwise, the kids won't touch them." Ariadne whacked obediently away, thinking of how Lois had "belonged" to Mama, how for Lois the belonging had merged into becoming until now Lois *was* Mama. Whereas for her, "belonging" to Daddy had been a dead end. What is to become of me? The wail sounded in her ears with fresh meaning: who is there for me to become?

Obediently she gave her attention to Peter and Reed when they dashed in with their prize possessions for her to see, but Lois flapped them away with the kitchen towel. "Go watch TV or something. Leave your aunt alone for a while."

"I don't mind," Ariadne said, "they're such darlings."

"Well, I do," Lois snapped, "I'll never get dinner ready in time with them underfoot."

Ariadne stopped chopping. "In time for what?"

Lois stuck her head in the oven again to say that they had theater tickets that evening—she and Emory. Her voice was muffled with guilt, but then she recovered the sense of deprivation, the resentment against life's injustices, the envy of her sister's beauty, the fine appreciation of her own hard lot that sent her into battle always armed with the might of right. She slammed the oven door shut and explained as to a backward and delinquent child, as if this had all been explained many times before: Ariadne could see a Broadway play any night in the week, but they lived in this god-forsaken hole and were lucky to get a lousy road-company on tour twice a year. So for once it was the original cast coming to town, they had scrambled to get tickets three months in advance, Ariadne had seen fit to wire them of her arrival just two days before. Lois supposed shrilly that she should have immediately torn up the tickets or given them away. Well, she hadn't. She did try to get another—impossible. Anyway Ariadne had probably seen the play, Ariadne had probably seen all the plays. So she had canceled the baby-sitter instead, it didn't make sense to waste the money with Ariadne in the house, but if that was an imposition? Lois threw the question like a gauntlet.

For a moment Ariadne let it lie there, then gave the demanded reassurance: it was all right, all right, all right.

"Don't give me that nobody-loves-me routine," Lois

said in disgust, "let's not get bogged down in that, for Chrissake. You always did go around feeling sorry for yourself, when the truth of the matter is you don't know what real trouble is."

Even trouble Lois wanted to grab. Only *my* trouble is real. Mine mine all mine. Ariadne wanted to laugh but was afraid it would turn out to be a cry. She fled through the swinging doors into the dining room. In the lower cabinet of the buffet would be the liquor. Above the buffet was a mirror, benignly approving, reassuring her in turn: it would be all right, all right, all right.

"If you're looking for the liquor," Lois called out, "I don't keep it there any more." At the thought of *keeping* liquor anywhere with Emory around, Lois barked a staccato laugh. "You might as well know—" but just now she begrudged Ariadne anything, even this confidence. The begrudging was thick in her throat even when she said instead: "I did get a bottle when I heard you were coming, it's in here."

She climbed up on the kitchen stool to grope in the highest cupboard, left the bottle on the drainboard with a frost-encrusted tray of ice.

"Mix your own," she grunted, "I've got to take a bath and get dressed."

Looking at the label, Ariadne felt the hard sullen core of her hurt melt away. It was an expensive, esoteric brand of Scotch—it was she who had raved about it on her last visit, had spent a whole afternoon trying to find in a local liquor store, had promised to bring some next time, had forgotten all about it. Lois, who didn't even like Scotch, had gone to all that trouble. For that, Ariadne forgave her everything, followed her upstairs, drink in hand, eager to spend its generous warmth on her sister.

"Tell me all about yourself," Lois shouted from behind the closed door of the bathroom. "Whatever happened to that lawyer you were going with—Jack, wasn't that it—or was that the one before? I know I'm awful about names, but honestly, Muff, by the time I've learned one, you write me you're going with somebody else, and it's hard to keep up."

Jack was the one before. Ariadne marveled at the meaninglessness of the name.

"Alan! That's it!" Lois called out in triumph above the raucous draining of the tub.

Alan. That was the name still with meaning. The one after Jack. The one before—whom? She fingered the angry red welts behind her ears as if they were some talisman for future peace.

"He sounds awfully young," Lois said, emerging from the bathroom, already girdled and modestly covered by a tailored slip. It occurred to Ariadne that she had not seen Lois naked since her marriage. Watching Lois slap herself vigorously with Eau de Cologne—it was more like someone being revived from a swoon than the application of provocative scent—Ariadne thought of their mother. She had used the same stuff—the genuine, original Cologne Wasser, from the same no-nonsense clear glass bottle with the old-fashioned black and white label that looked as if it belonged beside a shaving mug in a barber shop at the turn of the century. And it would permeate any dress Lois wore, Ariadne foresaw, wincing in advance of the loan sure to be requested.

"The kids are awfully quiet, aren't they? I'd better go see what they're up to," she offered, hoping to escape before she had to be generous. But no, Lois stayed her, peering shortsightedly at her tiny gold watch on the dressing table—they were watching Superman. Not Paul, of course. Thank God he had finally outgrown most things on TV. He was having supper and spending the night with a friend of his down the block.

"He wanted to call it off when he heard you were coming, but he's old enough to learn a little responsibility about engagements. A promise is a promise, I told him, you can't break a date just like that because something better comes along. Of course, I didn't know then you were staying just the weekend. He won't like that, he's still fond of you, you know."

"I know," Ariadne snapped, furious at this niggardly present of Paul's affection. Fond! He loved her. And she loved him. More than the other two, for she had lived nearby when he was a baby, spent almost every weekend here, baby-sat, was part of the family. For Peter and Reed she had always bought toys for the Two-Year-Old, the Four-Year-Old, but for Paul, she knew Paul, she brought presents chosen specially for him.

"I didn't know I was a date. I thought I was an aunt."

"It's the same thing," Lois said, obstinate in her righteousness. "Not that I expect you to agree with me. You would always break any date if someone you cared for happened to call—last minute or no. That kind of thing never pays, you ought to know that by now, Muff."

Rummaging in the closet, she found the two dresses Ariadne had hung up, fingered them like a canny shopper. Even as she admired them, she thought: God, the money she wastes on clothes! Her own shopping lists unrolled before her: things for the house, underwear for the kids, shirts for Emory, things for the house. Never anything for herself, anything *good*, like these. All the money she thus saved was transmuted by the heat of her anger into these extravagances of her sister. She chose the yellow linen shift, held it up against her. "Don't tell me what you paid for it, I don't want to know. Think I could get into it?" She had the dress over her head before she asked, "You don't mind, do you?" Flushed by the exertion of fitting into a size ten, she offered her children to Ariadne to feed, admitting it would be a great help.

They had been served by the time Lois came downstairs in the borrowed dress, with Adriadne's straw handbag over her arm, screwing tighter Ariadne's baroque pearl earrings on lobes too narrow to hold their weight.

"It looks fine on you," Ariadne forced herself to say, instead of stripping her sister naked and clutching her things to her chest. You've got to learn to share, Mama had always said, when Lois grabbed. But she's got Emory, the kids, why does she have to have my things too?

"Thank God for shifts," Lois said, "I couldn't get into anything of yours with a waistline." In the kitchen her eyes turned to the clock. Silently she removed the children's dishes, set two clean plates.

"Emory's late?"

"The 7:15 bus is the last that'll get us into town in time." A time-table offered with no further comment. After one phone call, to which there was no answer, Lois served their own dinner. The silence threatened to congeal even the steaming food. Desperately Ariadne began to talk, a river of talk into which Lois's curt sullen replies sank like stones. As if to make up for Emory's absence, Ariadne forced herself to confess to Alan's.

"He joined the Peace Corps. He's in Peru, working in the Indian villages."

And she heard how it sounded in this house, to her sister's ears. How far a man would go to get away from her.

"As young as that?" Lois asked, perking up.

"They take them up to thirty-five." Ariadne quickly made the point, even though Alan was far from thirty-five. They had told her the maximum when she had tried to join too. Even as she said goodbye to him at the airport, pressed against the wire fence like a displaced person caged in war's desolate aftermath, she had known he was gone for good. She had said goodbye to enough lovers to catch the intonation of a final farewell.

But even this gift of her own despair was of little use. Lois readied herself to leave, her face marbleized with rage.

"Maybe he's at the store, maybe he couldn't get away," Ariadne suggested. The words echoed, the scene shimmered, all this *déjà vu.* Or was it just that with each visit she found herself trying to defend Emory, to cover up for him, to feed him excuses—she who had never liked him. She could remember exactly how she felt when Lois told her they were getting married. Incredulous. "Surprised?" Lois had crowed, yes crowed, having kept this man secret, meeting him away from the apartment, giving no hint of him in their midnight accountings. As if Ariadne would steal him too, given half a chance. Looking at him then, his dull smooth face, his neat brown hair, his spanking white shirt, the precise geometric design of his tie, Ariadne thought: so this is what she wants, this man who looks like a male nurse, a dental assistant, a man of mean ambition.

Not that he hadn't surprised her once or twice. Like the night Peter was born. She had stayed with Paul until Emory got back from the hospital. His drinking had been acceptable that night—a celebration—besides he held his liquor well. She who got high on one drink envied him that. His speech was more precise, if anything, only his gestures, usually so tight, slopped over a little into expansiveness. He had taken a formal Victorian stance at the mantel, his elbow nudging Lois's wedding picture, to deliver an address on what he wanted for his kids. Not what she had expected—the College Education and all that. School was just something to get through without being blighted. It was after that life began, away from home. He would send them around the world—bumming, not touring. Dames, yes, dames —from the time they could first jack off, okay by him— but no marriage, not before the age of thirty. He forbade it, he absolutely forbade it, pounding on the mantel until he had knocked the picture down and Ariadne had giggled, on her second drink by then, "Such great ambitions, Emory."

She had another giggling thought now: nothing becomes him so much in life as the drinking in it, but Lois's look of cold contempt was sobering. She shouldn't have mentioned the store, she saw that now, remembering the telephone call that was not answered.

"Maybe he honestly forgot?" Ariadne said, then wished she had left out honestly.

"Honestly?" Lois repeated, leaning on the word with the full weight of her sarcasm. "Oh, he forgot all right. By the third or fourth or fifth drink, he can forget anything. Or so he claims. Well, you can tell him for me—" she stopped briefly to censor the instructions seething on her tongue—"tell him if he comes in time, I've left his ticket at the box office. Maybe he can catch the second act."

Yes, yes, Ariadne eagerly agreed, he would probably make it by the second act and she wouldn't let the kids stay up too late, and everything would be all right. She held the front door open, fiercely willing her sister down the walk. A purely evasive tactic, but it might postpone the fight until the morning. And then the kids would be around and they would have to wait again. And she herself knew how to maneuver between warring man and wife, an old skill once learned, never forgot.

"I wish," Lois called back, "I hadn't canceled that baby-sitter. Then you could have come with me. I hate going anywhere alone—I've lost the habit, I guess." She teetered in indecision, like an inexpert swimmer suddenly afraid on the high dive, until Ariadne shouted, "You'll miss your bus," and another habit made her run.

Released, the door swung to, Ariadne was alone. But then she had the habit of it. She heard no sound of the two boys, only the background noise of the TV, seemingly as much a part of the house as the creak of wood floors, the hum of a refrigerator. She missed Paul—he was old enough to talk to, to be company. It had not escaped her—that sly spiteful jealous maneuvering—sending him to spend the night with a friend.

"Just wait until you have one of your own," Lois used to say, at that time crediting the possibility. "Then you won't have time for someone else's, believe me." Even now Ariadne blushed to remember how she had rolled over and purred, like a cat being tickled in a particularly delightful place, as if Lois were *promising* her. Little Paul wasn't so stupid, he heard his mother right, heard quite clearly the grim warning of sure and imminent desertion. Hid when she arrived. Threw tantrums when she left. She could date the exact moment Emory and Lois had given up all prospect of marriage for her: Paul stopped being "difficult." Children hear everything, even though the door is closed. She heard it too, as clearly as if she had lain there too, crowding them closer together—the brutal judgment of man and wife in private deliberation side by side in bed.

"Do you think she still kids herself she's gonna get married to one of those guys?"

In the dark Lois would have pursed her mouth into

the mean shape of impartiality. "Well, some women do get married even in their fifties."

"Not your little Muffie, you can bet your bottom dollar." A tight man, Emory, who never bet his own. "She'll go along like this for a few more years, picking up these young kids, giving it away for free, until one day, when she 'confesses' how old she is, he'll have no trouble believing her, and boy, I hate to think what'll happen to her then."

And Lois would have defended her. "I don't see that it's so important she get married anyway. It's not as if she could still have children. *I* wouldn't take the chance at her age."

In the dining room mirror, Ariadne examined her face. Perhaps she should have let him change the nose, deepen the lids—but she had wanted nothing changed, just the same face, but all over again. The thought of all over again now frightened her.

She flushed out the children but tonight even they failed her. "Dogs and little children love you, you can't be *all* bad." Who had teased her with that? Emory? Jack, divorced, his daughter weeping for Ariadne when they broke up? She couldn't remember, it didn't matter. Brusquely she put Peter and Reed to bed, unable tonight to love other people's children.

She had just finished cleaning up in the kitchen when the front door slammed, announcing Emory's return. A look at the clock convinced her he must really have forgotten. A man late on purpose—in her experience—was just a little late, not so impossibly beyond the hour. Poor fellow, she thought, and put the coffee on to reheat. It was a ritual setting that mesmerized—she in the kitchen, he coming home from work (it made no difference that she didn't like him). She was flushed by the gentlest wifely concern, eager to comfort and console, when she presented herself to him in the living room.

She had forgotten about the TV—it was still on, although the sound was turned off, and the picture gave the only light in the dark room. He had fallen on the couch, eyes closed as if asleep, his face held toward the bright big eye of the cabinet like an onanistic sunbather working on a midnight tan. She turned on a lamp, and he raised his head to look at her, then let it plop back wearily. "Look who's here," he said flatly, his eyes closed again, making it out to be no surprise, not much pleasure.

Even drunk he was neat. He lay on his back, his legs stiffly aligned, his arms folded over his chest, his white shirt, open-collared and short-sleeved but convertible to a proper dress shirt, unwilted and unsoiled. His shoes were off, but placed together beside the couch so properly they seemed like some cherished belonging set to accompany his corpse on its funeral voyage. The kind of men's summer shoes she hated—of brown leather, heavily structured, but perforated with innumerable tiny holes for ventilation.

She wondered suddenly if he had passed out. Or even, was he dead? She had these moments of panic, witnessing the sleep of others, when it seemed to her she could see no rise and fall of the chest, no movement of life. Sometimes awakening at night beside her lover, she would listen for the sound of his breathing, hear none, and lie paralyzed with fear that he was dead until she willed her hand to reach out and test his warmth, feel his heartbeat. "Emory," she cried out, in a voice she might have used to pull him back from an abyss.

He opened his eyes, and turned his head, the rest of his body unmoving. "Don't look at me like that," he said.

She knew only gratitude to him for being alive. "Like what?" she asked and smiled tenderly.

"Like? Like. Like that old Gorgon's head, wrapped in curly snakes. I can see them, all those writhing snakes you wear for hair, their little flat heads arching toward me, with each forked tongue hissing love, love, love. Turn any man to stone. Any man."

"Oh, Emory." He was drunk. She shook her head, playfully rebuking him, the hair swishing into her eyes. "You *are* under the weather, aren't you. Where have you been? Don't you remember this was the night you and Lois were going to the theater?"

He stared at her, a deaf man laboriously reading lips.

108

"Where have I been?" he finally deciphered. She was relieved when he closed his eyes again. "A good question. White's? The Pink Horse? No, Joe's Bar and Grill. Corner Pine and Maple. Ladies especially invited. And every third drink on the house, don't forget that, that's a real saving."

Just as she concluded from the silence he had gone under for good, he startled her by sitting up, swinging his legs back on the floor. "Come on, sit down, I'll tell you all about it."

When they're in this condition, it's best to humor them. She sat down beside him, hands in her lap, ankles crossed, with the transitory propriety of a subway rider.

He stared at the wall opposite them, eyes squinting for focus. She thought of the two of them, side by side on the sofa, all ready for the projection of colored slides with accompanying lecture.

"So there I was." Slide please. Joe's Bar and Grill. "There was this girl, see. Beautiful? I'll say she was beautiful." As if Ariadne had just asked. "Man, she was a knock-out. Real honey blond. Hair straight down to her shoulders, and she kept swinging it around, swinging it around. A lot of that black gunk around her eyes, but nothing on her face, not even lipstick. A kid, nothing but a kid, and already in the business. Said she was nineteen, but that was a lie. You can smell it, you know, when they're young like that." He fell silent, his nose twitching, defining the smell. "Like they've been laying out in the sun, but a little sour—nice sour—like they're still wearing their bathing suit and it's not quite dry. Makes me think of when I was a kid and my folks had a summer place by the lake—"

"Emory," Ariadne said sharply, moving slightly away, feeling the sweat in her armpits, between her thighs. "You didn't—?"

"No, I didn't." But he was mocking her. "Not that I didn't give it some thought. It was her being so young. Guess I figured I could jerk it out of her into me. Then maybe I figured, what the hell, who wants it? Besides, it doesn't work that way, does it?" And when Ariadne said nothing, continuing to make little embarrassed

109

pleats in the hem of her skirt, his voice nudged her roughly. "Well, does it? You ought to know."

She could think of nothing to say. She shook her head, hair swinging, swinging back again to cover the scars.

"No, that wasn't it," he corrected himself. He linked his hands behind his neck, laid his head gently back, seeking the right answer now in the ceiling, the wall having failed him. "It was her bra straps. Her dress kept slipping off one shoulder and I kept seeing them—dirty gray, twisted, like something chewed with spit."

He was looking at her now, she could feel it. "You want to know why I really didn't go with her?"

"You don't have to explain to me, Emory—"

"Who's explaining? I'm telling. The price she quoted was a little too high." A grin slid loosely across his face, sideways and down and out. "Like Lois, I can remember when bacon was ten cents a pound."

He put his arm about her, but in a manner carelessly social, the brother-in-law. She relaxed, feeling she was to make her real entrance now, he would say, Well, Muff, old girl, and what's with you? But instead his fingers busied themselves with her dress. He said, "One thing I've always admired about you, kid, is your bra straps, always so neat and clean, makes me think of what little girls are made of." Angrily she replaced her dress.

"Lois uses safety-pins," he continued critically. "You're the pretty one, she always said, and damn it, she's right. She's not so right about being the smart one, though. If she's so smart, look at her, look at us, look at you. You're the smart one, too, if you ask me. No matter what else, you never had kids. That's what does it, kids. You can't leave the kids."

There was first the weight of his hand on her shoulder, then the weight of his head. She pushed him down into her lap (where he lay lost, lost—she could hear him crying into the creases of her dress for someone to show him the way out). Lois had whispered hoarsely, "We've got to talk," but she had not let Lois talk. She must not let Emory talk—not any more. (Although she knew the way out, she alone knew the way out.)

"You don't mean that, Emory," she said in short panting gasps. "You're just too close to see it the way it is. To know what you and Lois have together. You love her. She loves you. You just don't know."

"Do I? Do we?" he murmured into the hollow of her breasts. "Love?" He sighed the question, his breath warm and moist as a tongue.

"Oh, yes," she whimpered, her body arching. "Love, Emory, that's the important thing, love." His mouth closed hers, his tongue overrode her tongue, but her thoughts went on and on, defining love, claiming love, defending love, praising love, so loudly and persistently that even in that quiet wife-empty house she failed to hear the faint cracking sound from her new-made face.

Compensation Claim

Seeing his son before him again, Papa Joe stands up in his white duck suit, letting the Sunday papers slide from his lap, his face, between the whiteness of the suit and his thick white hair, sallow as a nicotine stain. Rhoda puts her arms around his neck and kisses him lavishly, imprinting on both cheeks a daughter-in-law's affection. Tall as she is, she can make it only on tiptoe and he hunches his shoulders to accommodate her. He makes no move to return the embrace, but stands with his arms hanging from the weight of age, like an old bull being garlanded with flowers. Then he reaches around her for Joe's hand, crushes it, encases it with his other hand, holding on as if to embed in his son's palm a secret message, not to be read in front of women.

The need for graciousness wells up within him, an urgent thirst. "Son, you got a treat coming," he announces gruffly. "I just brought up from the cellar a gallon of last year's wine, and it's the best damn blackberry wine I ever made. And I make the best damn blackberry wine there is." Only by the gruffness of his voice does he refer to the four vintages that Joe has not tasted, the four years that have passed since Bud's body was brought home for burial.

Joe still feels his hand between his father's hands; otherwise he would protest: drink wine in the mid-August heat? Instead he scowls back with the same ferocious expression of goodwill, being equipped with the same heavy brows, the same low sloping forehead, the same prognathous jaw that gives this Gavin face, so

112

faithfully reproduced in all eight children, an almost brutal anthropoid set.

"What did you think drove me back here, you old galoot, if it wasn't that blackberry wine?"

Louise looks across the porch at him with shy gratitude—a grayed woman, from whom age has wiped all distinctness, whose face, even as he stares at it, wavers before him, blurred, shadowy, unrecapturable as a dream: mother. Joe feels a familiar prickle of annoyance. The electric fan that ruffles Rhoda's red hair, then Louise's gray coarse waves, mechanically impartial, is his gift to her. The navy sheer she is wearing. Not to count all the tens and twenties he has slipped into her purse whenever she visits him. She has thanked him for each gift, like a shy girl remembering her manners; but now that he has spoken a kind word to Papa Joe, she thanks him with her eyes. When she turns back to Rhoda, presenting to him her left profile, he is startled by the tear oozing down her cheek. She who never cries! Then he remembers her trouble with that tear duct, an inflammation that has passed but leaving her, who never cries, with water constantly welling in the left eye, overflowing into a perennial tear.

Papa Joe is back with the jug-shaped bottle held in the crook of his arm. He pours half-full four water glasses, each of which he holds to the light to show the royal purple, squinting his eyes into thin slits of appraisal, arching his brows then in appreciation—brows black as coal under the white hair. His face suddenly appears to Joe as clownish, Chaplinesque.

"Damn good wine," Joe agrees and drains his glass, hoping at least for more kick that he remembers. These back porch visits depress him. Everything is so old, so broken-down. No piece of furniture is ever thrown out of this house; there is only a slow inexorable recession from front rooms to rear. The lumpy daybed is the one he and Matty slept on in the dining room. Those wicker chairs were on the front porch, not the back, when he was courting Rhoda. The old treadle sewing machine, gutted of its works, still serves here as a table, and on it Bud's last photograph in a silver frame—again the

Gavin face, dark brooding swarthiness of hair and eyes and heavy brows. But younger—the youngest of the sons, the one Papa Joe laid his hands on like giving grace —eyes looking past the camera, lights reflected in their blackness, shining dedicated eyes proper to one about to die so young.

What was it Papa Joe kept telling everybody at the funeral? The plane never got off the ground, it never even got off the ground, he kept saying over and over, as though there would have been no tragedy had Bud died in mid-air. But by the time they got back to the house, Christ, he was talking it up. Bud the hero, the solo ace of Papa Joe's war, not this one. You could just see the plane—like in those war movies, prewar style— paired wings as frail as the balsam slats of gliders you flew with a rubber band, laced together with struts toothpick-thin, and there in the cockpit, helmeted and goggled like he was riding a motorcycle, Bud going ack-ack-ack. Bud, for Chrissake, remember Bud, Papa? Joe had wanted to cry. He was my brother. But, my son! Papa Joe had wept, as if he had only one. And Joe had said—just what it was he said, he does not remember. He remembers faces that skew their mouths around, but no words, only Papa Joe's bellow of rage, that great barrel chest retching out its curses, and himself keeling not before the words but the hate, knowing it had been nourished under his father's tongue all those years, like smooth pebbles to practice eloquence upon.

Get out of this house—get out before I throw you out!

As if he too flinches from some memory, Papa Joe pours out quickly another round for just him and his son, the women too busy with talk of hem lines and hair styles, both getting longer. Rhoda's legs are pretty, she hates the thought of letting down her skirts, but her hair is pretty too and she may decide to let it *grow*, though long hair makes you look older, doesn't it? With the second drink, both men are overcome by a sluggish quietness, but Rhoda is always in a convulsion of affection enough to fill a silence. Sitting at Louise's side, she presses her hand and strokes into place, after each revolution of the fan, a wisp of the grey hair that is blown

114

askew. Louise submits stiffly to the caressing. It is Rhoda's way, not hers, to hug and kiss and stroke and pat. Rhoda is so tanned now that the countless little freckles hardly show and her red hair sparkles and snaps fire, holding the gaze of both men, while she discusses whether she should grow it long, now that chignons are in style. Louise suddenly rises. "Wait," is all she says, and goes into the shade-darkened house.

"We had better get along," Joe cautions his father, and Papa Joe agrees. But Louise is back now, holding a white cardboard box. She opens it, her face stiff, giving away no secrets, and from a nest of tissue paper draws out a flaming coil of hair that flickers like a living thing. "I cut it right after Bud was born," she says, and her hands hover over it, chilled hands cupping the warmth of a fire.

Rhoda screeches, "But it's my color, the exact color!" Only a woman's ear could catch the little stress of pique in her delighted surprise, and Louise smiles as she presses Rhoda back into her seat. At first slowly, the movements only half-remembered, then with increasing deftness, she twists and turns and pins the hair into a chignon on Rhoda's nape.

Joe stands gaping, stunned by the revelation, and Papa Joe roars, "You should never have cut it off, woman!"

Louise does not answer him directly, but through the pins in her mouth remarks to Rhoda, one woman to another, on the foolishness of man. "He's thinking that, left on my head, it would still be this color."

She gives a final pat and retreats to admire her handiwork. Rhoda crouches in front of Bud's picture and tries to trap her reflection against the protecting glass, but the dark dedicated eyes under the visored cap pierce her image. She dashes into the house to examine herself before a real mirror and they all follow, for Joe has looked at his watch again.

"McKettrick will be at my place about four," he says to Papa Joe, "and if there's any guy that can straighten out this compensation claim for you, it's him. He says there's one thing for sure, you ought to file an appeal.

It's all in how you present your case, and he's all set to give you pointers."

Papa Joe nods agreeably. He is one of those veterans who camped by the Anacostia in 1932, and he is ready to march against the Government anytime, on any score. Feeling almost buoyant at the prospect of a good court fight, he inspects complacently the whiteness of his duck suit in the hall mirror on their way out. Joe sneers at the archaic affectation of summer white, but Papa Joe feels it distinguishes a gentleman, as nothing else does, from trash.

The new car which Joe has been driving for the last three months is right outside. Papa Joe sees it now for the first time. Ever since the funeral, with Joe not stepping foot inside the house, Papa Joe has meticulously not stepped outside whenever Joe has driven by to pick up Louise. Only the two women have passed in and out of each other's house, as if with the immunity of neutral observers.

Joe has parked in the low-slung shade of the chinaberry tree and left the windows down, but even so, Rhoda gives a little scream as she feels the first burning touch of the seat cover against her stockingless legs. Taking the new highway to pick up speed, Joe whips up a breeze hot and dry as a desert wind. New cars are still hard to get and Papa Joe, leaning forward from his seat in the back to examine the dashboard, wonders how much Joe had to pay. "I hear these new cars ain't worth a damn," he says. Joe pats the wheel affectionately. "This one's a beaut. Hasn't been in the garage once."

"Pull your dress down, Rhoda," Papa Joe snaps, and settles back by Louise.

The air is cooler in the fashionable foothills of the North Side, and Joe has achieved the very crest of a hill for his new house. When he parks in front of the sprawling ranch-type structure, they see below them the entire city sparkling in the sun. "You should see it at night when it's all lit up," Joe says proudly, and leads the way inside for Papa Joe's first tour of inspection. Louise has reported all the glories, but Papa Joe is to see for himself at last.

116

"They tell me," Papa Joe says as he is led from room to room, "these postwar houses won't stand up—it's the green lumber they use."

"This one will," Joe says with quiet confidence, flinging wide the casement windows.

By the time they reach the children's room, Papa Joe is tired. His back aches, his knees trouble him, he can feel a headache coming. He would like to sit down, but all the furniture is scaled down to a child's size. There are two of everything: two rockers, two chests, two desks, two toy boxes. As they stand in the doorway, Joe examining the room with him, matching him in admiration, he feels his son's arm laid affectionately across his shoulder and the weight is more than he can bear.

"Wait until you see them when they come back from Rhoda's folks," Joe says, "you won't recognize the kids, they've grown so. It's about time we built an extra room —Rhoda and I feel that after a certain age each kid should have his own room."

The front door bell chimes melodiously and as soon as Joe leaves to answer it, Papa Joe desperately searches out Louise. He finds her sunken deep in the oversized couch in the living room and plants himself by her side. Stiffly he gets to his feet again when Joe ushers in McKettrick. Papa Joe inspects the small rotund man with the neat fringe of dark hair, baby-thin, around a bald pate, whose manner has all the earnest affability of the successful insurance man. Smiling down at him, aware of his own size, Papa Joe feels more at ease.

"What'll it be?" Joe asks, "Tom Collins all right with everybody?" McKettrick's nod is one of deep satisfaction, and Rhoda claps her hands, applauding the well-spoken line. Rhoda never sits properly, Papa Joe notices; now she perches on the arm of McKettrick's chair, idly swinging bare legs.

"Drat it, I clean forgot!" Papa Joe cries, slapping his knee in vexation. "I meant to bring along that gallon— a kind of housewarming present." He sticks his jaw out at McKettrick. "You ever taste homemade blackberry wine, sir?"

117

McKettrick makes a doubtful face. "Can't say that I—"

But Papa Joe has already started on his eulogy. Is hardly in full swing when Joe announces, "In lieu of anything better, here's to the juice of the juniper," and hands around tall cool drinks.

McKettrick strokes the pink top of his head and looks at Joe with a questioning brow. Joe gives a little nod of understanding and clears his throat cautiously. "McKettrick's the guy I was telling you about," he says to Papa Joe, "he thinks you can make a damn good case for that compensation claim."

McKettrick finds the introduction brutally abrupt and seeing Louise bring her handkerchief to her eye, he lowers his voice as he does when he speaks of the dead. "A tragic case," he sighs, "I remember having read about it in the papers at the time it happened. So early in the war—and such a needless sacrifice, too. Wasn't he just a member of the ground crew, had no business being in the plane at all when it took off? It must have been all the harder to bear, coming that way, so unexpected, so uncalled for."

A needless sacrifice, so uncalled for. So had Joe called it that other hot August afternoon, not with that smarmy tongue but bitterly, big brother bawling out the dead for being dead. And Papa Joe, tailspinning down to earth, had yelled Get out! Joe grips his drink nervously, Louise places a hand gently on Papa Joe's arm, ready to restrain. But Papa Joe is not angry. "A tragic case," he has heard this stranger say, and he leans forward, anxious to tell this man, who has clicked the roof of his mouth with sympathy, all about Bud. But Papa Joe is confused—the excitement of the reconciliation, the new car with no gears to shift, the new house *(Rhoda and I feel . . .)*, and now he wants to tell the story of Bud's death the way he always tells it, but the words do not come, only the sadness comes. It is like on Poppy Day, when he pins in his lapel the red ribbon of the Legion of Honor and makes a special trip downtown so that a pretty young girl may stand on tiptoe and pin by its side a red crepe paper flower in memory of

the war dead—then tears come to his eyes and he remembers the first line of that poem, "In Flanders field the poppies grow. . . ." And this is the way he now remembers Bud, like the sad first line of a patriotic poem.

Then words do come, in a rush, tumbling over each other, louder and louder, until suddenly he hears his own voice and falters, flailing the air with empty gestures, for he has been talking about 1917, and how he did not wait for the draft but volunteered, and how his thigh-bone was shattered in Belleau Wood, but he has remembered that this is the wrong war and the point of the story is that the plane never got off the ground.

He sinks back on the couch, and Louise takes his hand. As always when she touches him now, it is with clinical detachment, and he flings her hand away pettishly.

"Yes, yes," McKettrick murmurs foolishly, and then plunges into the heart of the matter. "Too bad your son didn't carry insurance," he says, shaking his head as an insurance man does, the reproof there but tactfully not insisted upon. "It should have been compulsory from the very start. However, this doesn't mean the government won't grant you compensation if dependency is clearly established. Now I understand he had made out an allotment to you—"

"Thirty a month," Joe confirms.

At the welcome sound of a figure, McKettrick unclips his pencil from his breast pocket and searches through the letters in his jacket for an envelope to write on. "It should be easy enough to prove that you can't support yourself without the continuation of that allotment. Let's see, your present income is . . .?"

Papa Joe shakes his head. "I don't understand," he says.

"That's simple enough," Joe says sharply. "There's your pension, seventy-five a month, and that just about does it."

"I don't understand," Papa Joe insists, "you're making it sound like I was dependent on Bud."

"That's the general idea," Joe says. "Anybody else

ready for another?" he asks, waving his empty glass.

"It's a goddam lie!" Papa Joe roars, getting to his feet. "Dependent be damned! Since when have I ever depended on a child of mine—or any living soul? Every cent I had I earned with these two hands, and if you think I didn't earn that pension, here's a bum leg that says I did. All through the depression—no relief check in *my* house, by God! Eight children we had—raised them all. Strong as an ox, every one, boy and girl. Good teeth." His finger shoots out triumphantly at Joe. "Anything wrong with your teeth?" he snarls.

"For Chrissake," Joe mumbles.

"Good teeth," repeats Papa Joe, thrusting out his jaw at McKettrick with such ferocity that McKettrick cowers deeper into his chair. Rhoda has stopped swinging her legs. "Eight kids. Where are they now? Married, with kids of their own, scattered over the face of the earth. They got no need for me, and that's okay by me, I got no need for them!"

Joe puts down his glass. "What about me?" he asks softly.

"You!" Papa Joe grins, a dry-lipped animal grin. "You!" (Why, the little bastard, Joe Gavin had grinned down at this first-born, sucking at Louise's breast, and the waves of that grin have rippled onward through forty years to break against the shores of this moment.)

"Yeah, me!" Joe shouts, "me! I'm still around. They all leave it to me to see to things. Seeing to things means seeing that your gas isn't cut off, your telephone isn't taken out, the house isn't sold out from under you for taxes. It means seeing that Mama has a decent dress on her back, it means—"

"You get out." Papa Joe's voice is so throttled with phlegm, Joe does not at first understand the words. "Get out!" Papa Joe yells now, "out of this house—and take that whore of a wife with you!"

Joe moves toward him, fists clenched. Then he stops and the fingers of his hands unfurl, and he smiles, almost tenderly. "You've forgotten where you are, haven't you, old man? This is *my* house."

Louise stands up at Papa Joe's side. She is afraid to

120

touch him, although he is trembling, but she stands close so he will know she is there. He turns to go, faces Rhoda, frozen into stillness on the arm of McKettrick's chair. With an incoherent cry, he leaps upon her and she screams at the feel of his burning dry hands on her shoulders, falls backward on top of McKettrick. Her bare legs and his immaculately creased ones become lewdly entangled. Before Joe can reach him, Papa Joe has pulled away. There is a skittering of hairpins on the floor and in his hand is clutched the switch of Louise's hair.

Forlorn, his love swallowed back like spittle, Joe watches him from the picture window, his tongue prying a crack in his dry lip for the savoury salt of blood. He watches Papa Joe reach the street and stop, not knowing which way to turn, with the entire city spread below him, a big man with shoulders hunched forward and crumpled white jacket hiking up in back, holding fast with one hand to an old woman weeping silently from the left eye and with the other grasping, like a fiery comet's tail captured from the sky, the inextinguishable beauty of her hair.

Stillbirth

Two blocks from the doctor's office, in the park, they lay together on proscribed lawn, considering the sky. Iona shivered, then blamed it on the grass, cool as a poultice in July's heat.

Hot and cold flashes, her mother would have said. It's your age, her mother would have said. You're the oldest, her mother would certainly have said; remember your age, don't hit Eddie, mind the baby, let Lois have the doll, help me with the wash. Hot and cold flashes, time of life. Iona wickedly let her have her say and then laughed; triumph wasted on a woman dead.

But in David's face she spelled out joy. His "What?" was high-pitched with incredulous delight.

"So you *have* wanted children," she accused him, welcoming the distraction of anger. "All this time, you've been wanting them."

His cheeks rounded high and hard in a grin, impudent as a squirrel's bunched with nuts. He rolled over and kissed her, denying everything but present rapture. That was David all over, to be perfectly content without a child, yet when presented with one to be just as content. How good all this is, he exults and then you give him something else and he exults with the same fervor: how good all this is. That was his charm, why everyone loved him; he taxed no one with envy. And so people gave him things. People were always perversely giving him things.

Now she was giving him a baby and how delighted he looked. Yet what did he know about babies? He had been an only child, not the oldest of six, pinned up in

122

mother's apron when the bedroom door closed on a woman stricken with strange fits. Time of life, they had told her, as if that explained all madness. Meaningless words. She had parroted them freely, shrugging thin shoulders.

Her father came in from the great male outdoors to shed the rough bearlike bulk of his overcoat, greet himself in the hall mirror with a look of bland, heavy-eyed, tooth-picking after dinner satisfaction. Armed with the shrug of outdoor maleness, he entered the dark stuffy closet of female madness and shocked them all with his presence. The stark black-and-whiteness of him. The black hair, the black brows, the cheeks, even when freshly shaven, steelblue as his razor. But underneath, everywhere, the white skin. An incredible opaque milky whiteness. Lips cut clear from the dark beard stubble, smiling bright pink. Beneath the black brows, eyes blandly blue.

A big black bear hug, a bright pink kiss he would give her. "A real little mother," he called her. Blandly one blue eye winked, winked at her behind the mother's back. Little mother. Her mother had called her that once too, and smiled, her upper lip feverishly dry, sticking to the teeth so that only the outer part curled away, giving the obscene effect of an animal's snarl.

Suddenly now, ten years dead, her mother appeared to her, flabby-breasted, paunchy, but with the sticklike legs and arms of the constitutionally thin, flushed with girlish radiance, her faded blonde hair curling with unseasonable sweat, smiling mistily, blondly frail as Lillian Gish. And ten years late Iona wept, knowing her guilt —her birth an inexorable sentence of her mother's death, all the years that intervened but a stay in execution, a long drawn-out waiting for the slow sure taking over of life itself.

"My mother," she said to David, explaining her tears. "I was thinking of her."

"I know," he said tenderly. "I think now of my father. As if for the first time I knew him, understood him, for the first time loved him as he loved me, as—" he patted her belly—"I love *him.*"

123

She took his hand, gripped it hard, like a child about to cross a dangerous traffic-heavy street.

"No, listen," he said, as if she had denied his argument before it had been voiced, "it's not blood or any germ cell, or that chromosomal stuff; it's this kind of love that is our immortal, undecaying, incorruptible part, passed from life to life like that sacred fire—Vesta's—that we must never let go out or there goes life itself."

She nuzzled her head against his and went "mm,mmm" letting the word love, love, love, lap over her like a warm wave. All the same, she smiled secretly, she could face facts and David couldn't—because he was only thirty-two and she was forty? because she was a woman and he a man? The truth was, he was just a child, a dear child. Love was the opium of children. The fact was the tyranny of death.

*   *   *

Mortal, corruptible, decaying, she dressed herself with extreme care, pinning her long blonde hair into a smooth French twist. Even in the dog-days' heat of this August, no bare feet in sandals for her, no shapeless shift. The black linen dress was formally structured and her long legs were encased gummily in nylon so sheer each depilated pore was revealed coarse as a pockmark.

"How do I look?" she asked anxiously.

Beneath the surface bubbled terror. A steaming geyser of terror, no Old Faithful erupting on schedule, but shooting up into consciousness any time, anywhere, so quickly subsiding her mind's shutter caught but a blur of its outline, leaving its recognition to the sure instinct of cold shrinking flesh. She looked down on the blue-veined topography of her hand. Mortal, mortal, her terror shrieked. She folded the front section of the *Times* and saw the month, the day, the year. It is now, her terror shrieked.

"Wonderful," David assured her, himself in open-collared short-sleeved sport shirt, thinking as he looked at her of mad dogs and Englishmen, but proudly.

"Wonderful," Moira Wilson declared, opening the door to them and then—freezing her into a monument—"How do you do it, Iona? You never seem to change. . . ."

Sucking in her stomach, Iona advanced into the noise of the party, the faces of friends bobbing like buoys in a heavy sea. When David left her side she floundered in unaccustomed shyness and stuck fast to the first group that opened up for her. She made her share of talk, drank her share of drink, but her eyes kept check on David as he passed from friend to friend, locating him each time he moved, like a poor swimmer testing for bottom. She knew the moment he gave out their news, thinking himself discreet in a corner, and sent out to him a telepathic message of hate for letting anyone know. And then the women came up to her, entangling her like seaweed in their welcoming complicity. The men began to whittle David down to papa-size with jokes.

"Yes, indeed, my boy, no more bumming around for you," a father of four decreed.

"No more uranium prospecting," an old friend offered.

"No more census-taking," another said.

No more racetrack policing, no more guiding tours to Europe; they turned the listing of David's odd jobs into a parlor game, making them up when they could recall no more.

Tension curling her toes in her patent pumps, Iona smilingly sat out the game, knowing that before the evening was over someone would have offered David a good job. Of the things people were always giving David, good jobs headed the list. And this time she knew he would accept it, as charmingly insouciant as when he had not. About making money, David *really* didn't care; not the way she did, finding in her big paychecks, pricked in tiny pinpoints, the sum of her worth.

A sudden ague of malaise shook her which even across the room David noticed. All solicitude he insisted on leaving immediately, refusing to listen when she insisted it was nothing, it would pass. She had to admit it was a relief just to be outside in the non-air-conditioned informal air, in the private night.

"There were just too many people there, I don't seem to be able to take crowds any more," she explained, but David still insisted on a cab.

Before he had flagged one she saw the still-lit window of a pastry shop. There, she pointed, giving a long ecstatic cry, she must have some, she must.

"Ladylocks, French horns, cornucopias—whatever they call them—those things with the cream filling. *We* called them ladylocks."

As soon as they were settled in the cab she tore open the little box.

"Only two?" she complained, "I could eat half a dozen." Not until she was well into the second, did she think to offer him a bite. "I haven't eaten these since I was a child. Daddy used to bring home six every Saturday afternoon and give them all to me—to divide, of course, after supper. Being the oldest, I could be trusted not to eat them all myself." Eddie, the little pig, she suddenly remembered. And started to make a funny story of it for David. "Eddie, the one next to me in age —" then left off to finish the pastry. But she repeated to herself: greedy little pig, recalling the times he had snitched hers. Lois she had first suspected, even little Joey. But no, it had been Eddie, of course. She could have strangled him with her own hands.

"They're delicious," she said, spluttering crumbs. "You should have had some."

David kissed a taste off her sticky fingers. Smiling, she licked the corners of her mouth, tidying herself like a cat.

"They made them much bigger in those days, and two for only a nickel," she said, then grew silent, regarding how time had dwindled ladylocks and made them more costly.

*   *   *

In the pale yellow light of a mild December pigeons preened and people basked with coats unbuttoned. Iona in her office revolved aimlessly in her chair, her shoes kicked off to relieve swollen feet.

126

Bill Cochran stuck his head in the door, smiled.

"Got your memo, see Eve on it, willya?"

His smile, she noted, jumped in wattage like a 3-way bulb: low in greeting but effulgent in departure. Mike Evans stuck his head in, looking for Bill and Eve. He gave her a mustached smile, reminding Iona of a rabbit twitching his nose in alarm. Later Eve came in and sat on Iona's desk for a just-us-girls chat.

"When is it due? I keep forgetting," she asked, although each day her eyes measured girth, making their own estimate. "So long?" She seemed surprised. "Well, it's those last few months that are the hardest," she said, always knowledgeable. Not until she was ready to leave, having jumped down and tucked her orange silk shirt into the slim waistband of her skirt, did she remember to say that Bill had passed on to her the memo. "Look, you've got enough to close out, I can take that off your hands at least," she said, generous in her parting smile. Iona kept smiling back. Behold the Cheshire cat, all those smiles dissolving her official substance like a chemical solution. There was nothing left of her here but a smile, stretching from ear to ear, slitting her face like a gaping wound.

Still revolving in her chair, flicking with each turn the papers on her desk, she was seized by a tremulous sense of levitation, an almost teenage giddiness, as if she were free-falling not through space but time. The ringing of the phone came from a great distance. Frowning over the loss of some great discovery almost made, some great decision almost taken, she picked it up and at the sound of David's voice felt an inner lurch, a loss of balance, as if she had braced herself to lift a heavy weight and it had turned out to be airy as a balloon.

"Let's drive upstate tomorrow, while this incredible weather still holds," he suggested with what seemed excessive exuberance, even for David.

She could see the trees in the little square below her office window, rusted with dead leaves which still would not let go. Her voice relaxed into a little whine.

"I don't feel up to driving through weekend traffic." For David she didn't have to smile.

"I'll do the driving," he announced triumphantly. "Got my license this afternoon. Surprised?"

"But I thought—just a minute, David." She looked down at the note slipped under her nose. Her finger darted out to click David off, then pulled back. Yes, she nodded, transfer the call to Eve Gilchrist, and briefly answered the secretary's smile. "I thought you hated the idea of driving—you know, having anything to do with machinery," she continued listlessly, doodling Eve Gilchrist's name on a memo pad and circling it over with elaborate curlicues.

"The thought came to me, light of my life, you don't have to love a car to drive it. Besides, think how the other kids will rag *him* if he has to admit his pop can't drive. I'll pick you up at five sharp. You'll know me by the old blue convertible I'll be wearing in my buttonhole. Ciao."

Strange to be sitting beside David at the wheel, as if she'd lost her customary place at the dining table or been ousted from the side of the bed that was always hers. She had to admit he drove well, with imperturbable patience; she recognized that patience. From the way his hands fondled the wheel he would end by loving the car, as she, who had never hated it, could never have loved it.

She caught him eyeing her at a traffic light, and raised her brows in mute question.

"You're getting to be a regular Jayne Mansfield—how do you like that, Busty?" he teased, referring to her own constant carping at her small breasts. Her face answered him with her office smile. He was not to know that since they had swelled almost overnight she could not bear to look at them, hated the heavy weight of them. These were not the breasts she had envied, these were milk sacs, no real part of her.

That night, in bed in a rented cottage, she remembered herself and wept as for a lost dear friend. The pale bloated body turning over with gravid clumsiness was not *her* body. It had been transformed into a swollen container, jostling its rightful owner; commandeered, taken over. She had long ago withdrawn from the outer boundary, that first line of defense, and cowered now somewhere within the inner flesh. Even there she felt the slow invasion as inch by inch *it* made its way. Inch by inch, gut twisted back on gut, stomach backed deeper into heart, kidneys squashed flatter against spine, bladder—the bladder soon would surely burst.

There's no more room, there's no more room, she sobbed in the darkness as inexorably it grew, shoving, kicking, elbowing, ramming its way. There's no more room, she whimpered, feeling the tautened skin of her belly like a thin sheath one bit more of tension would break. And still it grew in rapacious self-centeredness, the coiled incarnation of greed, greed, greed. She saw its image: on its face the features crudely lumped like half-risen dough, wearing the inward-directed smile, the ineffable smirk of Bhudda, lapped in the still waters of infinite wisdom, while all about it raged the storm of its survival before which the timbers of her body creaked and the fibers of her flesh were torn. Lying beside David, who slept, self-contained, she screamed for help.

"David," she cried. Then louder, until he awoke. "I'm not going back to work Monday." She decided it just then.

"Good," David mumbled.

"I mean, Monday or ever."

"Good," David mumbled.

"I'm getting too fat," she wailed.

He turned over.

"Take it easy, take it easy," he soothed. Whoever said she had to work to the last minute? Had she been picturing herself as the heroine of the *Good Earth?* As for her getting fat—true, she had burgeoned during the last few weeks—it was, he warned her, those damn pastries she kept eating—but, had he ever told her? he liked 'em fat.

Then he rolled over on his stomach and went back to sleep.

*   *   *

She could hear him stamping the snow off his boots on the mat outside, cursing at their neighbor's discarded Christmas tree still cluttering the hall. He came in, nose and cheeks red from the cold, dressed like a lumberjack from the great Northwest with huge buckled boots, ski jacket, fur cap with the earflaps down.

She began to giggle and found it hard to stop.

"It's the groceries," she explained. "The way you're dressed, that big bag of groceries looks a little out of context."

In answer he shouted:

"Mush!" and cracked an imaginary whip on his way to the kitchen.

When he came back he grabbed her hands and laid them against his cheeks to impress her with the cold.

"Man, it's great outside," he said, "you've got to come, right now, and take a walk. Just for a couple of blocks. It'll do you good, Iona, you don't get out enough."

She balked, making much of the cold. Inside she had arranged herself comfortably, but outside abysses yawned, eyes stabbed, a mirror in the shopwindow caught her unaware, crying shame. But after much coaxing, she consented. Following his cautionary directions she put on two sweaters beneath her coat, lightweight but a wrap style that could still be lapped across. She didn't bother with a handbag—David's pockets were munificent enough.

David looked at her doubtfully.

"Aren't you going to put up your hair or something?"

"I can't stand pins in it just now," she said, and tossed it back to clear her coat collar.

Secretly she admired it that way, falling long and blond and straight, held back by a black velvet ribbon. It was the only part of her now to which she gave much care, brushing it lovingly before the mirror, seeing only the hair and the face, which had rounded back—as if time were really a snake biting its own tail—to the face of that child whose mother's time had not yet ended, whose own time had not yet begun.

"Alice-in-Wonderland," he called her, laughing.

She held her arms tight against her body and closed her eyes, awaiting the inevitable pat on her stomach— crude punctuation of a dirty joke.

Head down, she followed David through the new snow, making a game of stepping just in his footprints, intent as a child not stepping on cracks, until the game was spoiled by a stretch of pavement cleared and graveled against the freeze. Before they could pass on there exploded onto the pavement, from a restaurant's privately chartered darkness, a wine-happy crowd, a wedding party.

Iona, like David, smiled at the shrill laughter of the girls, the embarrassed horseplay of the men—blue-serged boys they were. Beneath drab winter coats the girls' party taffetas stuck out like flowers bursting the seams of their calyxes, bent on blooming, snow or no snow. In that hot white glare of concentrated youth the eyes had to be adjusted before the old ones could be seen: two old couples, parents of the bride and groom.

Iona knew them immediately as such, flushed out of distant home towns, huddled together to one side, brushed, corsaged, and told where to stand for the occasion. She could tell they did not know each other; when they spoke, the women touched their corsages, the men considered their cigars. They were like background figures barely edging into a photograph, ready to be snipped off to improve the composition.

And indeed snapshots were being taken. First the bride and groom shot with rice, then uproariously with snow. The best man kissing the bride. The groom retaliating on the prettiest girl who swooned in mock ardor for the camera's eye. And then—of course they had not been forgotten—the parents were ushered front and arranged in a formal pose, flanking their progeny. Just as in the theater, Iona thought—ignoring David's jiggling of her elbow—when two stars and their supporting players, having sucked dry the audience of all due applause, graciously extend their hands to call front some minor character, a walk-on part, so that they and the audience may applaud each other for their magnaminity.

"I want to go home, David," she pleaded, her flanks prickling with terror, her hands oily with fear.

And he, thinking she was surely ill, took her home.

*   *   *

Even bouncing off pavement and the metal poles of lampposts, the rain that March night smelled of spring. A thick mist of fecundity swirled in the darkness, as if the gutters gurgling were rivulets wetting fields, as if the cracks in the sidewalk were sprouting up green.

Iona lay on the couch in the living room, dressed for bed in a baby doll nightgown which she had resurrected because of its loose fit. It was limp with age and near the hem, dangling at mid-thigh, a cigarette burn had eaten away a gaping hole. Across those white thighs the veins crawled like blue worms, gorged and swollen, burrowing under tattered lace. She watched the wash of rain down the glass, breathing hard but safe at last, wearing her hair long and free, eating ladylocks.

In the bedroom, still boxed and beribboned, the layette was stacked in a corner. At first, opening the door on David, she had thought the boxes all for her, being accustomed now to his little surprises. (Tonight, it had been the pastry. Although each day he phoned before leaving the office for the shopping list, usually he "forgot" the desserts she ordered, this transparent concern for her weight as sweet to her as any cake.) "Oh, David, for me?" she had cried, merely as a formula of surprise to hide her greedy delight—then she had seen the pink and blue lambs that gambolled over the wrapping. He had wanted to open everything for her inspection, but she knew well enough what baby things looked like; she told him she would have to empty some drawers first, they would only get dirty. He had brought them a week before her due date and now each day that passed she had the secret satisfaction of sticking out her tongue at gambolling lambs and David's foolish panic, being two weeks late so far, proving all along there was plenty of time.

132

I'll empty out those drawers tomorrow, she promised herself. Too lazy to move, even to bed, she watched David busy himself at their desk, doodling again with drawings which, from a distance, looked like an architect's blueprint. He refused to tell her what it was, covered it up when she approached, and though she played the game of teasing to be told, she was pleasurably tickled by the promise of surprise.

The first pains came, as David had darkly prophesized, while she was clutching a half-eaten pastry in her hand, her mouth encircled with crumbs and cornered with cream. She called out breathlessly:

"David," skimming the surface of her air supply.

He was too engrossed to hear.

She walked over to him, said "David" and looking up into her face, he knew.

"Put that down," he commanded, "you're not to eat another bite. And lie down. No, walk about, keep on your feet. No, for Pete's sake, get dressed."

Reluctantly she lay the pastry on the desk.

"It may be just a false alarm."

But then the pain came again. She dressed slowly, halting every few minutes to crouch over her own belly. Her arms were still thin, even stick-like, pathetic wrapping for that huge contorted bulge. She became almost grateful for the pain when it came. It was a feeling. Between pains, she had no feeling. She was breathless and her heart beat fast, but she noted this as a memorandum for future emotion, just as she noted David's frantic scurrying to shave and his funny (she noted it was funny) surveyal of his entire wardrobe as if there were something suitable to wear for such an occasion.

Waiting for him, she gripped the edge of the desk, smearing his drawings with the crushed pastry. Meticulously she tried to clean off the mess and while he raced downstairs to flag a cab, her eyes followed the ruled lines, the arcs for doors, the cross-hatches for windows, the outline of furniture drawn in and labeled.

Not until she was readied in the hospital gown and perched on the high hospital bed, with David beside her again, looking ill at ease, as if expecting instant ejection, did she remember to ask:

"Those plans on your desk, David."

"You peeked," he accused her, but laughed, finding it hard to bottle up anything, even surprises, spilling it all out in relief.

On the white bed sheet, he drew out the nursery of his plans, partitioning their bedroom with carefully thought-out carpentry. She watched his finger move along the whiteness, emptying the room of her belongings as the room of the newly dead is emptied and aired and rearranged for a new roomer.

Starched white skirts brushed her, the needle pricked her arm, the doctor said something to David, his voice low, conspiratorial. They spoke together, men's voices, shutting her out. Like a sack of laundry she was rolled onto the cart. No! she screamed, as the walls of her room, *her* room, leaned perilously forward and the ceiling drooped down in plaster festoons.

She ran screaming to escape that fatal press, ran down a long dark corridor. There at the end was a hole of light, like the promise of a tunnel's mouth. She labored forward, but when she reached it, there was Eddie, with his monkey's grin, and behind him Lois. They were all there, all five of them, even bare-bottomed Joey. With joined hands they formed a ring, barring the exit. She ducked under their arms, only to be imprisoned in a dancing circle she could not break through. The sinews of each child's arm were woven strong as hemp, binding her closer and closer as the circle of dancing narrowed in.

The press of their bodies became unbearable. No, she screamed, and ducked out again, running back through darkness until she saw the other mouth of the tunnel and the little hole of saving light. But there it stood, huge-headed, monstrous, teetering on its tiny stump of a body, curved and blue-veined like a shrimp. Head lowered, it seemed intent only on itself, listening to its own heartbeat. But from under the bulging bald dome she saw the sly slits of its eyes upward turning toward her and the corners of its mouth now scarcely contained its smile.

No, she screamed, and whirled, but even the long worm of darkness had coiled in on her. Eddie walked toward her, tow-headed, snub-nosed, his face split with a smile of perilous sweetness. Holding out a paper bag, he called:

"Here's six ladylocks and they're all for you."

For a moment, the air seemed lighter. She stopped, breathed. Reached out an arm quivering in exhaustion like a plucked violin string. Then remembered.

"You devil!" she screamed, "you know I mustn't eat anything!"

And before the inexorable advance of his sweet offering, she turned to run again. But there was the head. Nothing but head. Bald, white, enormous, bloated head. Filling the exit, filling the whole tunnel, and now, lowered like a bull's, it plowed through the darkness to the attack. There was to be no more running. Pressed against the wall, she closed her eyes and felt the shock of its ramming. No! she screamed, no, no, no. The cord, pulled tight, fitted like a noose when the last grinding down of terror tore her free and set her afloat on a softly lapping wine-dark sea.

The Meat Eaters

You would never have thought, looking at them, that meat was so important a part of their diet. They were tall and thin and faintly blond, more like sister and brother than husband and wife, and both spoke in the same soft apologetic mumble as if ashamed of their size. Their droop, their drawl, the tired flickering of their colorless eyes under glass brought anemia to mind, yet it would have been hard to find a more carnivorous pair: bacon or sausage for breakfast; liver, kidney, sweet-breads, brains for lunch; the roasts, chops, steaks for dinner. They liked pork, beef, lamb, mutton, poultry. They liked rabbit, venison, and partridge, and were hoarding, just in case, recipes for bear, whale, and rattlesnake.

It was Michael who suddenly would not eat meat. Almost five, their son had inherited their blondness, their tallness, and, for the first three years of his life, their appetite. "A real gourmet," they complimented each other as he licked the paté off their crackers and wolfed down their own elaborately sauced entrées minced into baby-sized bites. But then, overnight, he would take nothing but peanut butter or American cheese.

"He looks perfectly healthy to me," Lowry said, when Anne first consulted him. "But then you know best."

As a husband Lowry was all that Anne desired, but as a father he sometimes failed to satisfy. That hesitancy in taking over, for example. Her own father had been trigger-happy with judgments. He knew how to raise daughters and he knew how to raise sons. Hypothetical sons. Red pepper ground into her thumb had stopped the sucking. Cold showers had doused her sister's temper tantrums. He had been against permanents and orthodontia. Coeducation he considered desirable only for boys. He had been for piano lessons, camp summers, pen pals abroad. With a boy it was different, he always concluded.

Anne would have known just what to do with a daughter. She would have reached back into her own girlhood as a woman reaches into a capacious handbag crammed in disorder and pulls out the lipstick, the car keys, the kleenex, the lollipop. But when she had folded back the receiving blanket, lifted the flannel gown, unpinned the diaper and saw, between the mottled thighs of her new child, the tiny deflated toy balloon of his maleness, she had received a shock from which she had yet to recover: I can't handle this, the thought had exploded.

He grew, and when she weighed him on the scales, she was the mother triumphant. But with any crisis, the old conviction of incompetence returned, unmanning as those fits of stuttering that used to seize her as a child.

"He bit me!" she told Lowry, who would know what to do, being a man, having been a boy. Michael was three. She had looked at the deep imprint of his two front teeth on her finger, had retched, had reached the bathroom just in time. He bit to reach the bone! was all she could think as she cooled her forehead against the ungiving marble of the tub and tried to stop shaking. She could never think of teeth on human flesh without her skin crawling. Once, in her teens, she had been trapped in a car with an over-ardent date. Pinned under his full weight, she had closed her teeth on a knuckle, a male hairy knuckle. She could no longer remember the name or the face, yet she knew that boy with an intimacy deeper, more ineradicable than any backwash of intercourse. She would always have in her mouth the feel of those black tufts of hair, the taste of salt acrid flesh. Not even to prevent rape had she been able to press her teeth into that flesh. Instead she had gagged, and vomit had served her equally well.

Lowry had seemed only mildly impressed by the aberration she reported.

"But biting, Lowry—*biting?*" Girls did not bite, but perhaps boys did?

"What does Dr. Spock say?" Lowry asked, leaving her again with that vague sense of disappointment, ill-defined and difficult to pin down, like certain cases of mild indigestion. And all Dr. Spock could think of to say was not to bite back.

The biting subsided, but then came the guns. A new world opened out before Michael. With the intensity, the concentration, the persistence, the whole-hearted passion they had learned to fear, being helpless before it as before some catastrophic upheaval of nature, Michael refused to play with anything that did not resemble a deadly weapon.

At this Lowry was more appalled than Anne. "I don't approve of a gun as a toy," he informed her stiffly, after she had purchased the first one. "I don't want him to grow up believing war is a game." Anne admired the way he put his foot down. The gun was "lost," and not replaced. But then Michael used sticks. "They're the same thing, but more dangerous," Anne found it necessary to bring up. "The way he runs, he'll fall on a pointed end and put an eye out. I'd rather he have the plastic kind."

Defeated, they took turns loading Michael's new guns with caps and winced at the noise and watched aghast as the arsenal grew: the pistols with gun belt studded with plastic bullets; a samurai sword (metal edge sheathed in rubber); bow and arrows (suction-capped); rubber knives; a pirate's plastic cutlass; a plastic Winchester that would really shoot—"remember, Michael, you are not to *aim* at anyone."

Were it not for the half-erased graffiti of another darker time—those faded orange and black "Fallout Shelter" signs—the question might not have arisen. But Michael asked and Lowry answered: those tall, steel-framed buildings had once been marked as shelters, he explained, from the excesses of nature, such as big winds and heavy rains. After Michael was in bed, and they had gorged on tripe à la mode de Caen (always a success now that Anne had learned to seal the casserole with raw dough so that the entrails could simmer languorously for hours in the white wine), the subject was broached as delicately as if it bristled with all the embarrassments of sex.

"You know, we'll have to tell him sometime," Anne said, clearing the table. "God knows what he'll pick up from other kids in nursery school."

Lowry took off his glasses, as he always did when faced with a difficult question, and contemplatively sucked on the frames.

"Look darling," he finally said, "you know where I stand on telling kids the truth. I have never lied to Michael, nor asked you to. It's just a matter of timing, that's all." It amused him that she still called it the Bomb—not ICBMs, not cruise missiles, not MIRVs—as if nothing had changed since her own childhood when those orange and black signs were fresh and the warning systems were tested every day at noon. He smiled with the tender superiority of a husband who not only drives the car but knows the engineering principles of the internal combustion machine. "We'll tell him when he's a little older, when he can understand without being frightened. Let's say, when he begins to listen to the news."

"I suppose you're right, dear," Anne said, her doubt betrayed in a leaky sigh. Her own reluctance to enlighten Michael was rooted in a different fear: that he would demand a toy Bomb—one that would really work. She decided to let the subject drop and ran the hot water for the dishes, leaving Lowry to suck silently on his annoyance. Whenever Anne was faced with a difficult question, he observed critically, she immediately stirred up a storm of housewifely busyness, as if hoping to dust the issue away or wash it away or polish it away or stack it away.

This was as far as they ever disagreed, and then only because the mother spends more time with her child (Anne reasoned) and a man knows his son as no woman can (Lowry believed).

"If by that you mean I can't identify with Michael as you do, that's true," Anne admitted. Lowry had a way of regarding his son as himself, reduced according to age and size, like a recipe halved but with all ingredients kept in proportion. Yet at Michael's age, his own passion had been for music and he was already recognized as a prodigy, if his mother were to be believed. Anne had written to her in a light vein of Michael's obsession with guns, hoping to evoke similar reminiscences of Lowry's childhood. Instead his mother had written: I do remember Lowry trying to play the piano at three, he always loved music and hated rough games and loud noises. I don't think he ever gave me a moment's trouble. I don't want you to think I was anything special in the line of mothers, it's just that he was probably born that kind of child and when I read the papers today I realize how lucky I was.

"Your mother thinks Michael's a juvenile delinquent."

"Don't be silly," Lowry said, reaching for the letter. "Where does she say that?"

Anne gave a delicate snort. Disregarding everything his mother said, she was still disconsolate. Boys are like that, she had wanted to be told.

"I *was* precocious where music is concerned," Lowry said, "but so is Michael. Look at the way he demands over and over again that old Kipnis recording of Boris Godounoff."

Rather, Anne objected (but only to herself), look at how he waits on tenterhooks for Varlaam's account of the taking of the city of Kazan:

> A young gunner crept towards a barrel filled with powder,
> The barrel began to roll. Oh! it rolled down into the tunnel,
> Yes! and exploded!
> The cruel Tartars shrieked and yelled,
> With inhuman cries they burst out screaming.

140

> An innumerable host of Tartars was wiped
> out,
> Wiped out were forty and three thousands
> of them.
> That is the tale of the city of Kazan.
> Aye!

"Yes, Michael has a good ear," she agreed. (Even with the words in Russian, he no doubt heard all forty and three thousand Tartars die screaming.)

Anne knew better than to air such suspicions, for Lowry was tender to the touch where music was concerned. Twice a year he played his own compositions, beautiful examples of sixteenth-century counterpoint, before selected friends and the few professional musicians of their acquaintance, after which Anne served skewered chicken with an Indonesian sauce of hot peppers and ground peanuts and lime juice. Before the performance, he would be manic with a sense of accomplishment, romping with Michael as he rarely did, trading bang! for bang!, kissing Anne with a blind nervous ardor. But for days afterwards, even when the praise had been lavish, he would be cold, removed, depressed: he had so much more to learn, and so little time.

"Think of Charles Ives," Anne encouraged him, "selling insurance helped him to write music and writing music helped him to sell insurance—didn't he say that?" Charles Ives was the only one she could think of.

"I knew what I wanted to do back in college," Lowry berated himself, "I should have switched majors, I should have gone ahead and been a starving music teacher, if it came to that." Since, with motherhood, her own career had dwindled to giving piano lessons at home, Anne winced a bit there. "Maybe I could have gotten a grant or a fellowship. I didn't even try."

He was not a man to drink, or he would have gotten drunk. Instead he huddled over the bowl of English walnuts, cracking the papery shells between the palms of his hands, flicking the unwanted nut meats to her. As she witnessed his Sturm und Drang, her love, dissipated into the little pools and eddies of familiarity, gathered

141

itself and swept over her again in full tide. Torment faceted him like a fine diamond; she reached out greedily.

"Do it now, darling," she urged orgiastically, "do it now!"

As they might have spent an evening among travel brochures planning a Caribbean cruise, they would plan a new life, jettisoning responsibilities like crystal glasses smashed on the hearth in mad Russian gaiety. Always they ended up in the kitchen, levitating toward a special midnight snack—scrambled brains it might be —and at table, they would reach out, with mouths full, to clasp hands, and it would be their left hands, their right hands busy with forks, so that beneath the warm intertwining, ring scraped coldly on ring.

"What other woman—?" Lowry would sigh rhetorically, mistily blinking his appreciation.

Not for one moment did they really forget Michael, who could be counted on to wake them the next morning by bouncing wildly on their bed. Then they gave him extra fierce hugs, as if to make up for the brief deprivation he had suffered while he slept. Those guns he would outgrow, Lowry promised Anne, but music would be a part of him forever.

"He *is* a sensitive child," Lowry said now, as if that explained the new eating problem as well.

Anne's face stood pat, noncommittal.

"Mother says when I was about five, I wouldn't touch meat for weeks, for just that reason. It's the first grim bit of reality a child has to face, and Michael finds it hard to stomach. I wouldn't want him any other way, now would you, darling?"

No, if Michael had been that way, she would have been content. If he had shed one tear, she would have been happy. She would have coped gladly with vegetarianism for a few weeks, even months, carefully balancing his diet with beans and cheese and milk. But all the time he had been asking questions, the same questions over and over, his appetite for meat had never flagged. Not then. She could see no emotion at all on his face, only the placid rhythmic movement of his mastication, the impenetrable brightness of curiosity in his eyes.

"What's this?"

"Why, you know, Michael, your favorite meat—lamb chop—and look, dear, I've cut off all the fat."

"I know that, stupid, but where does it come from— the baa-baa kind of lamb?"

"Michael! Do you remember what I told you about calling your mother stupid?"

"The baa-baa kind?"

"Well, yes."

"What part?"

"Oh, do start eating, Michael, you dawdle so."

"What part?"

"This happens to be from the leg."

He was not only eating it, he was cramming his mouth over-full, so that it took him forever to chew and swallow. But he never allowed that to interfere with his mealtime conversation.

"What am I made of?" He held out his leg and looked at it curiously.

"Bone—and flesh."

"What's flesh?"

"Well, it's like meat, but with people we say flesh."

"Will you eat me when I am dead?"

"Michael! Of course not! Of course not!"

"Why not?" As if he could think of no earthly reason why not.

"People don't eat people, and stop chattering and eat your—of if you've had enough, there's chocolate cake for dessert."

Thank God, that line of questioning had finally been dropped. It was she who suffered the after-effects, not Michael. She held a whole chicken in her hands, took practiced grip on the thigh, slit with a sharp knife just through the skin, rolled the bone in its socket, twisting until the muscles tore, the tendons snapped. Not until the leg came free in her hand was she aware of her stomach sucking itself in and heaving upward, gagging her like that male hairy hand she had once mouthed. She dropped the chicken, the dismembered leg in the

143

sink, raised her hands to her face and almost passed out from the stench of raw fowl. From then on, she had her chickens quartered by the butcher.

Mealtime with Michael was all hers, but Lowry had shared in Michael at the zoo, an experience that should have ruled out tender-heartedness forever as the source of any of Michael's problems.

"Michael, do look at the monkeys, see how they use their tails to swing!"

But he would not be moved from the lions and tigers. Monkeys bored him. No teeth. At least no teeth like a lion's to tear flesh. No, meat—animal meat, human flesh. Meat we eat, flesh never. Never? No, never, never, never.

Wistfully she had watched two little girls in the Children's Zoo, so sweet in their spring bonnets and buttoned patent shoes, stroke tenderly the soft fur of the rabbits, pat the nubby blunt brow of the adorable lamb. Michael would only clamber over the Noah's Ark, pretending it was a pirate's ship. "Oh, do look, Michael," she called to him, pointing out the little girls with the lamb, but he wouldn't even look. On the way out, he stopped in front of the lamb for a moment, considered it gravely. Buoyed with a great hope, she took his hand; patiently, as if teaching a blind child braille, she drew it over the thick springy wool. "Isn't it cute?" she murmured.

Released, he made no effort to repeat the gesture. "Which leg do the chops come from, Mommy?" he asked.

She laughed wildly, thinking: At least his vocation is settled, he'll be a butcher, we can cut out all those refinements of education we have planned.

Lowry saw none of this. He liked the big cats himself. The panther was his pet, and when it paced its cage, Lowry watched the undulation of its haunches and sighed, "Beautiful!," the moist steamy passion on his breath mixing with the fetid animal stink of the cages and turning Anne faintly green.

Guns and daggers, bows and arrows, saber-toothed tigers, Tyrannosaurus rex—the fiercest meat eater of them all. You're pretty old, Mommy, will you die? Never. Never? No, never, never, never. Questions of death and dying, death and killing. Death and eating.

Anne did not notice exactly when the questioning stopped, but it had been some time ago, before he stopped eating meat. "How long can he live on just peanut butter and American cheese?" she demanded of Lowry until "Maybe you're right," he agreed, "see what the doctor says."

Dr. Tilsit was young and reassuringly scientific. He did not remember Michael from one check-up to another, but even this was reassuring, lending to his final judgment all the credibility of a double-blind study.

"I can tell you right now there's nothing wrong with this child," he shocked Anne by saying after one quick look, but then restored her confidence by making a careful examination and suggesting certain tests.

"This one will cost you a small fortune and it's money down the drain," he said cheerfully, wrapping thin rubber tubing around Michael's upper arm.

"It's too tight," Michael complained, "don't twist it so hard."

"It has to be hard to be good," Dr. Tilsit guffawed. "Now this needle's not going to hurt like a shot does, Michael. Does he get upset at the sight of blood?" he asked Anne.

"No," she answered, trying to ignore her own queasiness. She had once donated blood to the Red Cross and they had had great trouble locating the vein. But the needle slithered into Michael's easily. Anne was proud of him, he took it so well, quietly watching the red liquid pool up in the vial. The only trouble came when the nurse stoppered the vial and took it away. "It's *my* blood," he raged, "they've got no right to take it away!"

Alone with her in his office, Dr. Tilsit repeated his assurances. "I'll phone you if the tests show anything, but it's not likely you'll hear from me. And don't get upset over his diet. At one time or another, the eating habits of all children are bizarre, to say the least. You can give him vitamins again, if you want to, but it's just money down the drain. What you may have here," he added thoughtfully, rubbing the hand that Michael had bitten, "is a behavior problem."

Even that would probably straighten itself out. If it didn't, he would put her on to someone in that field. He didn't say so but Anne could see that he felt it would be money down the drain.

She met Lowry downtown for lunch, and as soon as they were seated in the restaurant, made her report.

"You see," he said, and tapped her triumphantly with the menu, "I knew the boy was all right. You brooding mothers, you're all alike. Now relax and enjoy yourself —the mixed grill here is delicious—and I'll call the office and take the rest of the afternoon off, just to celebrate. Would you like that, Michael? Shall we go to the zoo?"

Michael agreed with a screech of delight.

"Not the zoo," Anne interjected quickly, "maybe the museum, where all the knights' armor is, Michael."

"That's even better," Lowry agreed. Recalled to the menu by the impatient rustling of the waiter's pad, he ordered two mixed grills and—consulting quickly with Anne—one American cheese.

They waited in silence while the waiter collected the menus and left.

"And what did you do this morning?" Lowry asked, his voice bright with interest.

"I—" Anne began, then realized he was speaking to the child.

"I went to the doctor, stupid." Michael said.

Anne moved the sugar bowl away as Michael dribbled the white powder from a torn packet on his tongue. Giving himself a fix, she thought with exasperation. "Yes, dear, but your father means before that." And added that he should not call people stupid. "You played with your friend Jason, remember?"

And which one was Jason, Lowry made the mistake of asking.

"Oh, you know, Lowry," Anne spoke up quickly, "the very blond, sweet-looking child. Small-boned, with beautiful coloring. Like a Gainsborough, although I suppose that'll change when he gets older."